RIP

Rhinos in Peril

Tim Moxley

To Mavis,

In loving memory of
Denis and Lydia
May they RIP x

Love and Laughter always.
Love

Tim x
Moxley (2017)

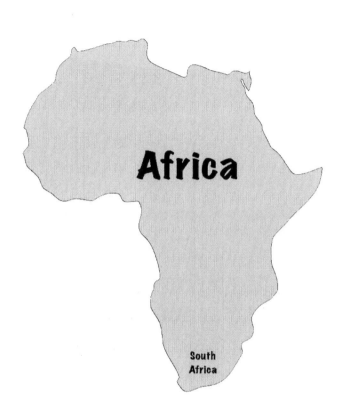

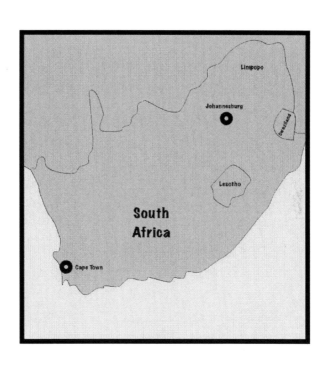

RIP Introduction

Rhinos, or rhinoceroses, as they should be called, are one of 'The Big Five' and are peace-loving, vegetarian creatures who tragically are top of the hit list for would-be poachers due to the growing demand for rhino horn as an aphrodisiac, medicine and symbol of wealth, particularly in Vietnam and China.

The statistics are dramatic and potentially catastrophic with numbers falling from over a million in the 17th Century to around 70,000 in 1970 and around 28,000 today.

I was offered an amazing opportunity to travel to South Africa to find out more and this forms the story of R.I.P. as we see it through the eyes of Ted and his three sons: Harry, Rob and Tom.

All proceeds from this book will be donated.

Together we can save a species.

RIP Chapter 01

Heathrow was as manic as ever. The baggage handlers had decided to take an extended Christmas break and the pilots were on "go slow" which Tom thought may mean that they were going overland to Africa!

The four of them could hardly believe it. Ted had recently retired and decided to take his trip of a lifetime with his three sons while he was still vaguely capable of enjoying it and possibly out- running or hobbling a charging rhino or buffalo. He was the player of the season at walking football and he did have three able-bodied strapping lads to help and protect him.

Ted smiled as they checked in on the computer and his youngest son Tom did a fake robot walk in honour of the baggage handlers.

"We want more pay! We want fewer computers or our jobs will be...exterminated!" His Dalek drone rang out across the terminal building. Ted shushed him and glanced around nervously. Hopefully nobody had heard his number three son or he would have to be seen to put on his teacher voice and pretend to reprimand him, instead of smiling proudly and laughing inwardly.

This was to be the trip of a lifetime. Three holidays in North Wales and one memorable one to London seemed tame compared to this adventure to South Africa.

Ted was hoping to start a new chapter after the tragic and untimely death of his beloved wife Rosie two years ago and early retirement that year. South Africa was the obvious choice for him. It was somewhere new, exciting and scary. These were adjectives that summed up day to day life as a widower and retired teacher.

His dad had been stationed there in the Army and always raved about the people and scenery and culture, though he refused point blank to discuss his actual war-time experiences.

His oldest son Harry was fresh out of university, heavily in debt and unable to find a suitable job. He had thought long and hard about a Gap Year to travel and experience the world, but this was even better.

The Bank of Dad could fund his trip and if he liked it, new opportunities would surely follow. Rob was 20, disillusioned by the fact that he had not made it as a professional footballer and totally knocked off track by the sudden and tragic loss of his mum. South Africa, he hoped, might help to re-define and re-motivate him.

Tom was 16, fresh from the dreaded GCSEs and still harbouring ambitions of becoming a journalist or writer. Another continent; new horizons; plenty of fascinating history and hopefully endless topics to write about and explore; it should be ideal for Tom too.

RIP Chapter 02

The rhinos were the main reason for the trip. Ted had been tempted by the glossy brochures and their persuasive descriptions of Cape Town and the Garden Route, with spectacular scenery, wonderful wildlife safaris, historical tours of Robben Island and the Road to Freedom, but he wanted to explore the real Africa with his sons and an invitation from an ex-colleague, Ellie, had swayed it for him.

She had volunteered on a wildlife conservation project in the Limpopo region north of Johannesburg and had fallen head over heels in love with the place, the people and more precisely, the rhinos!

They had met up at Chester Zoo and the energy and enthusiasm that electrified her eyes and whole being when she talked about "her rhinos" came across immediately and Ted was hooked. He had read up and researched 'Rhinos in Peril' and had been shocked and stunned by what he discovered.

Hundreds were being slaughtered every week for their horns and at the rate it was happening, they could be extinct by the time his kids were his age.

He had been an Art teacher for nearly forty years and neglected his talent for painting, but had been so moved to act that he had produced a series of paintings entitled 'Rhinosaurus' depicting vulnerable looking beasts which were half rhino and half dinosaur. Even Harry had been impressed by his pun to hint at their possible future extinction.

They would meet Ellie, visit the Reserves, volunteer on a Rhino Project and he would draw and paint, Harry would write about the history and culture to use in a thesis for a future M.A. Course and Rob and Tom could use up their endless energy by helping the owners and interns and producing blogs and websites to publicize the plight of the rhinos.

Ted and Harry were convinced that they could make a real difference by raising awareness, educating people and raising much-needed money by selling paintings and books. Tom and Rob were sceptical as always, but looking forward to a good holiday, lots of laughs and no more emotion as they were all cried out.

They hadn't counted on the rhinos...

RIP Chapter 03

The flight was long and gave plenty of time for contemplation. Ted tried to concentrate on reading but was constantly distracted. He pretended to read the 'In Flight' magazine. He was more interested in the couple in front who were rowing about everything conceivable. It ranged from whether you got fewer pretzels in a bag these days to whether a Toblerone was better or worse with less jagged peaks to draw blood from your gums.

He tried to guess what job each passenger did from their clothes and demeanour. He decided that he was surrounded by an accountant in a pin-striped suit reading the Financial Times; a nail technician complete with fake tan and multi-coloured cuticles; a teacher with huge bags under their eyes and worry lines who was reading a self-help manual and a social worker with a permanent fixed grin and vacant look playing the game 'Hay Day' on her mobile phone.

He studied the rather overweight couple by the emergency door. They clearly needed the extra leg room, but might get stuck in the emergency door or on the chute if a real disaster was imminent. He wrote pen portraits in his head about each of the stewardesses and made pencil sketches of them in his notebook, too cruel and caricatured to show them.

Harry tried to sleep, but with no success. It was an overnight flight, but whenever he was dozing off he was offered food or drink or dodgy Duty Free tat. It was difficult to believe that a baby behind them who was clearly on Duracell batteries could howl for so long.

Rob and Tom played a number of games ranging from 'Mancala' to the more intellectual 'I Spy' - but as always their competitive edge caused ructions and Ted had to give them his best teacher "death stare" to silence them.

In the end they resorted to watching the Flight Movies though 'Sully' where Tom Hanks miraculously landed a plane on the Hudson River and 'Castaway' which opened with a plane crash were not ideal choices considering their location!

Ted watched Will Smith in 'Collateral Beauty' and found it moving and thought-provoking, but a bit too 'Hollywood' in its ending.

How would he and the boys react to their African adventure? As the plane touched down in Johannesburg in searing temperatures, he was about to find out.

Rhinos, here we come...

RIP Chapter 04

Johannesburg Airport was a nightmare! It reminded Ted of break duties in the school Diner, but on an even vaster scale. They had to queue up with hundreds of others to have their mug shots and fingerprints taken, just in case they were going to get up to any of their old Scouse tricks!

They were delayed even more by the young man in front of them who really puzzled the immigration officers by not having any fingerprints. It turned out that he worked in the pineapple industry and pineapple juice erases your prints - a handy tip for would-be burglars!

Finally they were out into the searing heat, searching for a friendly face amongst the scrum of taxi drivers and travel reps until they eventually picked out Ellie.

Soon they were heading for their base for the next couple of weeks in Limpopo in the north of South

Africa, close to the Zimbabwe border.

The drive was fascinating in itself. South Africa was a vibrant, buzzing country full of different and unusual sights, sounds and smells.

The countryside as they left the airport was like North Wales, but with sun. The rolling hills and beautiful greenery were reminiscent of Snowdonia but what made it very different were the street vendors who lined the motorway. Ted and family were nonplussed by them but their driver explained that they were selling chargers, mobile phones, in fact anything that could earn them a few rand.

The roads were straight and in good condition, at least until they were forced to take a detour along a dirt track through villages with a market place, where a succession of black faces scrutinized them and watched them go by.

As they travelled further north the scenery noticeably changed and so did the vehicles on the road. There were much less hire cars and private vehicles and more vans and trucks, often piled high with fridges, microwaves and washing machines which they were taking over the border to Zimbabwe to sell.

The mountains were much more dramatic, particularly the Drakensberg Range which were really impressive and the greenery of further south became much redder and browner.

The heat had become more intense too and typically the air conditioning in the car decided to play up.

Toto's 'Africa' and songs from The Lion King and Paul Simon blasted out from the car radio and for once the whole family, even Tom, were silent, wondering at the scenery and lost in their thoughts, contemplating individually what lay ahead.

Tomorrow, the rhinos...

RIP Chapter 05

The camp was a haven in the South African bush. It was exactly what Ted had expected and hoped for, but a bit of a shock for the boys.

There was a central lodge which consisted of a large stone floored sitting and dining area with an array of comfortable chairs and recliners and a large kitchen with its own larder and storage area. There were two living areas which were traditional African rondavels with high domed thatched roofs containing a huge cooling fan and a circular base which housed six beds. Each had its own bathroom and toilet from B&Q's Rustic Range.

There was also an outdoor swimming pool and outdoor gym and a large grassy area for resting, sunbathing or eating alfresco under the African sky, which was full of stars.

They were met by their host Christo who greeted

them warmly and gave them a guided tour and briefing.

Tom, as usual, was full of questions when he had completed his introduction and the answers were interesting, if at times, slightly alarming.

"Why is it called Buffalo Camp?"

"Well, I hope you don't sleepwalk, or, if you do you're a fast runner. We share this camp with the resident buffalo and let's just say that they have the right of way and they are not as friendly as us."

"Are there any snakes or scorpions?"

"Yes and yes, though nobody has died yet, but we do have requests from fathers with over-inquisitive sons."

Ted smiled and nodded appreciatively. Tom predictably asked:

"What about internet and Wi-Fi?"

"I'm glad to say the answer is no. The nearest town is twenty miles away and you can get coverage and reception there, but this is the Bush and so, unless you have got a trained carrier pigeon or Hogwarts owl you'll be out of the social media bubble for a couple of weeks. There is no malaria problem around here but you may be suffering from the dreaded FOMO when you get home."

Ted beamed at the news. He was forever nagging his sons about their obsession with their phones and I pads and how antisocial it made them.

"The art of conversation died when Tim Berners-Lee invented the World Wide Web!" he had declared on a number of occasions in a monologue, because his children were busy texting OMG or LOL to their friends.

This was going to be a real eye opener for the lads and he hoped that it would bring them closer together as a family and help them rediscover and reinvent themselves.

"Now I suggest you unpack and get some sleep. Breakfast at will be at 4am tomorrow morning and then we'll be off on our first drive. You will get to meet the real stars of this camp and the reason we are all here. The rhinos..."

RIP Chapter 06

The temperature had been hot! Mosquitoes had buzzed around and caused concern. They had obviously had enough blood during the day to not bother with midnight feasts.

They had all slept reasonably well, though they had dozed rather than gone into a deep sleep, such was their excitement about what lay ahead.

Four o'clock had never really existed for any of them before and they were all dazed and confused as they munched on their breakfasts. None of them were hungry, so had to almost force down the food and make their jaws work, knowing that they would need the fuel later.

They were given a further briefing before they climbed on board the white bakkie; a 4x4 Jeep crossed with a Land Rover. It had two spaces in the cabin for the driver and spotter/navigator and two raised benches on the back, which would seat four on each row, so eight in all.

"Watch out for low-hanging branches, unless you want a permanent wood tattoo as a souvenir of your stay. Duck or grouse," Christo told them.

"Keep your hands inside the vehicle at all times and keep your voices low, but if you do see anything, let us know. You are all eyes and ears and have a vital part to play in the drive. If there are any questions, don't hesitate to ask."

Ted gave Tom a knowing look as if to limit his questions to the hundreds, not thousands.

"Don't leave the vehicle until we tell you that it's safe. Then walk in a single file and don't make any sudden movements."

Rob was tempted to make a joke about not monkeying around, but for once decided against it.

"Remember that in a zoo, animals have been captured to live in a human environment, but you are here in the animals' environment so they will see you as either a threat or an unusual gourmet dinner. Always respect that environment, respect the animals and behave in an appropriate manner."

Ted hoped and prayed that his sons had been listening as intently as he had. At least they had Ellie with them, who had done this drive hundreds of times before and that re-assured him.

"Now make sure your water bottles are filled and your brains are tuned to Bush mode and we can go and find the rhinos..."

RIP Chapter 07

The scenery was amazing. As far as the eye could see, the bush vegetation was dotted with green thorn acacia bushes and mopane trees.

The family had been told about the native baobab trees, but they had to be seen to be believed. The guide books described them as "grotesque" which couldn't be further from the truth. They were truly beautiful and seemed to have characters of their own. All had distinctive shapes and sizes. Some trees had vast trunks - which suggested that they were hundreds of years old.

The baobab trees' smooth bark was fibrous and apparently used for making floor mats. Its powdery pulp was also rich in Vitamin C and used within high energy drinks - which were, allegedly, healthier than the Red Bull drink.

Hearing these details reminded Ted of when he had confiscated a can of Red Bull from a student during his class registration. Instead of throwing the can away, as he said he had, he sampled it to find out its effects.

Following the drink, Ted had never been more productive in his teaching. He talked as if he was stuck on fast-forward. He also felt his heart pounding, as if he was running in the Olympics.

"If only they could talk, what stories they could tell," thought Harry wistfully as they drove past another incredible specimen.

"Hopefully these baobabs, which will long outlive us, will not witness the destruction of a species. I hope and pray that they do not live to see the last rhino die." Christo's voice trailed away and the whole family was transfixed by the rich emotion and genuine love in his voice as he spoke.

"That's why we are here. We are Mutogomeli, as the

Afrikaans say. In other words, guardians of the six glorious, precious white rhinos on this reserve and our passion is to track them, check on their whereabouts and well-being twice a day, every day, to ensure their safety."

"Do you get poachers then on the Reserve?" Tom chirped up, but was silenced by the withering stares of both his dad and Christo, simultaneously.

"The answer to that question is a key one, but for another day. We want you to enjoy your first wildlife encounter and first experience of South Africa without getting too hooked into the gruesome, gory and tragic horror connected."

Tom was more intrigued than ever but knew that he would have to be patient for once.

"So let's go and meet the true heroes of this project. The rhinos..."

RIP Chapter 08

The drive was the most incredible experience of all their lives. People had talked about the Bushveld providing a truly spiritual experience which had left them all cynical and sceptical, but they were about to have their minds well and truly blown, their gobs, well and truly smacked. Christo sat up front with their driver and extra guide for the day, Neil, one of the founders of the initiative, with the knowledge of a native Bushman and a teaching style which Ted really admired. Ted, Harry, Rob, Tom and Ellie filled the back of the bakkie, variously dressed in what they considered to be Safari garb. They had all made the effort to choose greens and browns, apart from Rob who had to wear a Liverpool shirt. Fortunately, Rob had been persuaded to go for the black away-kit, rather than the Day-Glo, fluorescent number which would have either scared off the animals or made him next on the menu.

Tom had been given a fetching Safari hat for

Christmas by Becky, one of his best friends, complete with bee-keeper face cover netting which he insisted on wearing, more for comedic effect than protective purposes, but today nobody really cared, such was their excitement.

Their bones shook as they headed along the track; dusty, ridged and rutted, making a red dust cloud as they progressed towards the boundary fence and out into the Bushveld wilderness.

The scenery was dramatic and awesome but it was the abundance of wildlife that really took them by surprise. They had expected to drive for miles, scanning the horizon for elusive sightings or even just glimpses of animals, but instead there was simply one amazing sight after another.

Ted had thought a lot about eternity and life after death, fervently believing that there must be another dimension or another realm and this was as close to how he imagined the Garden of Eden to be. Yet here the animals didn't come in two by two, it was more like twenty by twenty!

The cares and concerns of life at home disappeared in an instant and it was almost as if their brains tuned in to a new frequency of a radio station they had never listened to before, but this was 5G with surround sound, smells and sights and even touch and taste.

Their senses truly came alive in a way they had never imagined possible and Ellie, who remembered the self-same responses from two years ago on her first drive, smiled to herself and counted the number of "wows", hoping to contact the Guinness Book of Records later.

And they hadn't even seen the rhinos yet...

RIP Chapter 09

"Altogether there are 120 species of bovid, 84 of which we call antelopes," Neil explained in his Irish drawl, "and everybody tends to have their favourite. Which one they like best is supposed to say something about the person's character and outlook on life, according to African culture."

Ellie loved the impala which were generally tan in colour with a brown saddle and vertical black stripes down the tail. Whenever a vehicle passed, it seemed to be party time for the impala, as they jumped high in the air, competing with one another for the highest jump, like an antelope Olympics.

Tom asked why they were behaving so strangely and was shocked by Neil's answer.

"They are trying to impress any potential predators that will usually pick off the weakest first, as 'easy meat'."

Ted had heard the expression 'easy meat' hundreds of times before, without knowing its origin, but now it made sense.

"They are extremely friendly, sociable and charismatic with a sense of adventure and love of roaming."

Rob preferred the waterbuck, which were much stockier in build with a long body and neck. They were coarse haired with a neck mane and ruff and were grizzled red-brown with black legs and a white rump patch and a distinctive elliptical ring around their rump.

"The ring looks like a toilet seat," Rob had remarked, "though I've no evidence for that. I've nothing to go on...unlike the waterbuck."

They always made people smile, but were rather more secretive and less confident than other members of their family, though they did have an innate strength and dependability.

Harry liked watching the impressive nyalas, which always seemed to be fighting whenever they passed. The females were bright chestnut with torso stripes and spots and chevrons on their chests. The males were dark charcoal grey with tan lower legs and a white spinal crest. They were seemingly aggressive in outlook, but it was all a show of force in order to survive and cope with life in the Bush. As the eldest, Harry had had to be the pioneer and leader and sometimes a show of aggression was necessary, though it was only for show.

Tom's favourite were the kudu. They were the second tallest, which he was in the family, with the most spectacular horns. Their heads were small, with huge, cupped ears because they were always observing and good listeners. They were red-brown to dark grey, with torso stripes and a prominent white nose chevron. They tended to wander round in groups, but males would often wander off and enjoyed their own company.

Ted was awestruck by the elands, which he had never heard of before. They were enormous beasts and more like an ox in antelope's clothing. They stood tall at over 60 inches high and weighed in at an impressive 2000lbs. or 942kg. They were tan in colour with torso stripes and white legs and the males turned blue grey as they aged. Outwardly they looked fierce, but they always tended towards flight, rather than fight and they could certainly run incredibly quickly for their size. They had a short neck, but incredibly broad shoulders and almost a haunted, soulful look, like they were carrying the burdens of the whole world on their shoulders.

Ted empathised and hoped and prayed that short term flight would help him learn long term fight. If antelopes were this impressive, what would their reaction be to the rhinos?

RIP Chapter 10

On the first morning they drove across the Reserve, pausing to take in one incredible sight after another. Giraffes tried to stare them out, wildebeest were seen running from the sound of the vehicle. Countless animals were pointed out to them by Christo, Neil and Ellie. There were aardvarks to zebra, with plenty of letters in between.

The sounds of the Bushveld really entranced them as well. The only sounds assaulting their senses were animals calling and thousands of birds chirping and chirruping. It was unbelievably peaceful, but at the same time cacophonously noisy.

Their mission each day was to track, find and monitor the six rhinos on the Reserve. Poaching was a major concern with over 440 rhinos killed every year in South Africa alone; one dead rhino for every 19 hours.

Christo bombarded them with facts and statistics as they made their way across the Reserve.

"In 1895 there were only 20 white rhinos left in South Africa, but thanks to huge conservation projects, including our own, numbers recovered to 25,000. Since 2007, mainly due to a huge increase in demand from South east Asia and Vietnam who believe it can cure hangovers and even cancer, poaching has increased by 8000% and numbers have fallen so dramatically that if it continues at the current rate, there will be no rhinos in the wild by the year 2030."

Ted was dumbfounded. He had done some research before their trip and knew there was a problem, but this was devastating news. Potentially, by the time he was 70 and his boys were in their 30s, the only place they would be able to see rhinos would be in an enclosure at Chester Zoo or wandering "free" at Knowsley Safari Park!

"The full name for a rhino is currently rhinoceros, but in our lifetime it may have to be changed to rhinosaurus."

They had been following the main track for about twenty minutes, but now took a sudden left turn and headed up the hillside, through ever-thickening Bushveld. The "road" became very rocky and they all began to understand what the term "bone-shaker" really meant, as they gripped the rail tightly.

"Ok, it's time to climb." Neil announced. "This is called Venda 1. Tom, can you carry the telemetry bag, please? When we get up there, we'll show you how to use it to find out exactly where our rhinos are having breakfast."

RIP Chapter 11

The rocks were red and highly polished and at times they had to scramble over loose scree, so their ascent was hazardous at times, but they followed Neil and Christo, in a single file, along an escarpment until they found themselves at the summit of Venda 1.

The view was breathtaking. As far as the eye could see in every direction was bushland with occasional acacia, baobab and mopane trees. They had been climbing in Snowdonia, while on holiday in Wales, on a number of occasions and were accustomed to panoramic views. This was different though. Civilisation was nowhere to be seen and as their eyes adjusted to their new surroundings, Neil and Christo pointed out wildlife sightings, which would have caused quite a stir in Wales.

"At two o'clock there are a group of elephants, charging through the Bush."

Before their "wows!" had left their lips, buffaloes were spotted and then giraffes, elands, zebras and impalas.

"Listen carefully! Anybody know what that animal is making that sound?"

They all strained their ears and caught the sound of a low growl, almost like a human laughing. Christo mimicked the call: "He, he, he..!"

It was a lone hyena calling to its clan.

"Striped hyenas are solitary animals that tend to live and hunt on their own, whereas spotted hyenas are more sociable and gather together in groups of up to 80, called clans."

Harry decided that he was more striped than spotted, while his brothers were definitely the opposite.

"Right, enough sightseeing, who wants to have the first go at tracking the rhinos? Ellie, as an experienced telemetrist, would you like to demonstrate while I explain how it works?"

They unpacked the telemetry set, which consisted of an aerial and a radio transmitter.

Neil explained:

"'Tele' in Greek means 'remote' and 'metron' means 'measure', so we are going to measure how remote our six babies are, at the moment, so we know which direction to head in, to track them and feed them. Each is fitted with a collar around its leg and we have to listen for a bleeping sound which will get louder and more distinct as we get closer. Right, Ellie, show them how it's done."

Ellie climbed to the highest point, held the aerial aloft and turned a neat pirouette of 360 degrees, listening carefully to ascertain when the beep was loudest and then fine tuning on short range when she was confident of the general long range direction.

"RB1 two bars at 3 o'clock from the bakkie," she announced. The boys looked suitably confused after hearing the jargon.

"Any guesses? Do we have a budding James Bond or Sherlock Holmes?"

Harry couldn't resist having a go.

"Rhino at location B1 on the map, east from our vehicle."

Rob had been silent and joke-free for ages, so chipped in:

"Richard Branson the First has been spotted by the paparazzi in two pubs, smoking ready-rubbed..."

For once it wasn't just his dad who gave him the Jackson death stare.

"Back to the bakkie," Neil said, "I'll explain on the way. Rhino Bull 1, meals on wheels are heading your way."

RIP Chapter 12

The bakkie made its way along the dusty, bumpy roads in the vague direction of three o'clock. The scenery was different to anything they had ever experienced and the bird life and wildlife sightings were frequent and awesome, but the anticipation of seeing white rhinos in the wild for the first time was the dominant emotion.

They stopped every couple of miles to check the signal on the telemetry and this caused them to re-route several times, but as the signal got louder, the excitement rose.

Finally, after what seemed like an eternity, Neil stopped the vehicle, checked the signal again and announced:

"We are on Band 5 now. That means they are nearby...very near." Tom and Rob scanned the Bush but could see nothing.

How could such a huge beast manage to hide so effectively? From what they had heard about poachers and the threat of extinction, it was through necessity rather than choice.

"We will continue tracking on foot," Neil announced.

Tom jumped to his feet and began to descend towards the ground.

"Not you! Rhinos are easily alarmed and when they are scared they generally opt for fight rather than flight. That's why a group of rhinos are known as 'a crash'. Their eyesight is really poor, but their other senses are acute, particularly hearing and smell. They will definitely have heard us by now and will be listening and waiting. Christo and I will go closer alone. They know our scent and so will not be spooked. Once they get to know your smell, they will be fine with you too."

Rob pretended to sniff his armpits as if offended by

the comments, but Neil and Christo had already gone, heading deep into the Bush with the telemetry aerial held high.

Ted, Harry, Ellie, Rob and Tom gazed around at the incredible scenery and felt the intense heat of the newly risen sun as they waited patiently to see what would happen next.

After a couple of minutes, they heard a cry of "Come, come!" and there was a rustling of undergrowth and Neil and Christo re-appeared about fifty yards ahead on the road and walked slowly and deliberately towards the bakkie.

Behind them trooped three obedient rhinos, almost walking to heel like they had been trained by Barbara Woodhouse, the famous dog trainer.

They had seen rhinos many times in zoos and Safari parks, but would never forget their first sight of these incredible creatures in the wild. They had an ancient, almost eternal, beauty. Their bodies were awesomely huge at almost six feet high and the earth shook as their three and a half tons trotted towards the onlookers. Their bodies were clad in what appeared to be thick folds of prehistoric body armour and their legs were as solid as tree trunks, covered in deep creases and folds.

Most impressive and memorable of all were the rhino heads. Their ears were immense, shaped like irons, but constantly assessing their surroundings and moving around like antenna. The telemetry kit, the trackers carried, was incredibly clever but God had equipped the rhinos with something far more accurate and sensitive.

The rhino eyes could barely be seen as they were hooded, but looked sad and soulful - almost haunted. When the spectators looked further down the rhino's head, they began to realise why...

RIP Chapter 13

The rhino's myopic eyes were set either side of their enormous heads. In the middle of the face, where all the previous rhinos had a magnificent scimitar horn, there was merely a stub. The second largest land animals in the world looked forlorn and emasculated.

Ellie remembered her first sighting, months ago, and tried to assess the reactions of her friends. Ted was staring almost dumbfounded, Harry was shaking his head, Rob had looked away and was pretending to tie up his boot-lace and as for Tom - she was sure she could see tears forming in his eyes as he tried to take in the scene.

The first sightings of truly jaw-dropping natural wonders, such as Niagara Falls, Mount Kilimanjaro or the Grand Canyon, are said to be 'spiritual'. Such views elicit so many raw emotions that the human brain can't comprehend. Words cannot describe. This was one of those experiences.

Leopards and lions are awesome sights and truly beautiful; elephants are impressively huge and almost comic in appearance; giraffes are ungainly and awkward looking - as if God had decided to show his sense of humour in their design. Buffaloes are imposing, monstrous and demand your respect, but rhinos?

Rhinos had a strange, haunting beauty and grandeur which literally took your breath away. They were trotting out of the Bush almost obediently, but there was no doubt at all who was in charge and who was almost trespassing on their territory. Yet their missing horn spoke volumes to everybody who had the privilege to visit them and share a moment in time with them. It was as if they were so deeply wounded and hurt by their treatment that they came out of hiding, in the Bush, because they wanted the world to know and react.

Rhinos are vegetarians and a threat to nobody or nothing and yet they are in mortal peril because of their crowning glory, their horns.

Ted, Harry, Rob and Tom knew in that instant that they may be seemingly powerless to change the situation themselves, but they had been recruited as rhino evangelists and like the Ancient Mariner in Coleridge's poem and Jesus Christ in the New Testament times, they would be compelled to pass the message on to everybody they met. The gospel of what conservationists, like Christo and Neil, were achieving in spite of the danger and lack of funding.

Rhino was short for rhinoceros and could never be allowed to be a simplified version of rhinosaurus. This moment was stored in their memory banks for ever and they were all determined that their friends, future family and indeed all the world should at least have the opportunity to share their excitement and awe.

RIP Chapter 14

Three rhinos had emerged from the Bush and followed Christo and Neil dutifully towards the bakkie. They looked at ease at first, but the nearer they got to the vehicle, the more nervous the rhinos appeared.

Christo later explained that the rhino eyesight was so poor that they could only make out shapes and not details, so they were comfortable with the shape of the bakkie, but aware that something was different. That was why it was so important to remain seated and avoid sudden movements or any noise.

They nudged and nosed the vehicle as if checking it out while Neil offloaded a bale of fresh hay to feed them. Tom was drawn again to their sad expressions and could not help staring at their hornless heads with a teardrop-shaped pattern of pink, white and black keratin where the horn used to be.

As always Tom's mind was reeling and formulating endless questions, but the sheer wonder of the occasion silenced him and he stored the questions for later.

The rhinos hungrily devoured their breakfast while Christo and Neil keenly observed and photographed them, giving them the once-over, like a daily check-up or MOT.

As soon as the food was gone, the rhinos sniffed the air, walked slowly around the vehicle, almost like they were doing their own checks and then trudged away, back into the dense undergrowth. The noise of their trampling was deafening at first, but soon faded and they were all amazed how quickly and completely they disappeared from view.

Everywhere fell eerily silent. It was difficult to take in fully what had just happened. It seemed impossible to believe that other humans were probably doing exactly the same as them, except instead of hay they were delivering bullets and carrying machetes.

According to statistics, a rhino is killed every ten hours, every day, in South Africa.

Neil finally broke the spell by announcing:

"Time to move on. Three down, three to go."

The rest of the morning was a blur for all of them. Seeing their first rhinos in the wild had been such a moving experience, that they were all numbed for some time.

The sun was getting hotter and it was a beautiful morning, with deep blue sky making the greens, reds and blacks of the veld even more vivid. They saw countless birds and animals. They managed to track and feed the other three rhinos, who were at a waterhole, close to the mine dumps.

Somehow it was all surreal and more like a dream than reality. It was almost like their under-used city dweller senses had hit overload and the only way to cope was to shut down.

Before they knew it they were back at camp and clambering down from the bakkie. They were all elated but exhausted and it was only eight o'clock!

"I suggest you grab some breakfast and then get some rest," was Neil's advice. "If there are any questions after this morning, I would be more than happy to try to answer them."

Ted smiled as he thought about the inquisition Tom would be bound to lead.

RIP Chapter 15

The family were to become accustomed to their new Bush routine. They were up at 4am for their first game drive to track and monitor the rhinos. They were arriving back for breakfast between 8 and 9 o'clock. Then there was free-time to rest, read, swim or explore.

The 'second-shift' of rhino-watch between 4pm and 8pm included the sundowners' celebration. Arriving back to camp for evening meal, which was usually a barbecue, or braai as they call it, and then to bed. It was hard to drag yourself away from the campfire and delicious food, but necessary in order to be rested for the next day.

Day one, however, was confusing. It felt like teatime, but it was breakfast. They had done their day's work but it was barely sunrise. They were hungry, but didn't really feel like eating.

Ted grabbed some cereal and settled back in one of the loungers which overlooked the swimming pool. It looked out into the Bush. There was a single acacia tree ahead, with the sun brightly glinting through it - an iconic African image. To the right was a huge baobab with gnarled trunk which almost seemed to be watching him and smiling at him. If only baobabs could talk. What a story they would have to tell of endangered species, now extinct? Species they had seen such as dodos, Atlas wild asses, bluebucks, Cape lions and red gazelles? Surely rhinos were not to be added to that list?

As Ted glanced over his shoulder he was stunned to see what his sons were doing. They were so full of life and energy that he expected them to be larking about, laughing and joking. Tom would be cornering whoever was available to bombard with questions. Instead the boys were all sitting silently, lost in contemplation and staring at the horizon.

Eventually Neil joined them and shared the photos he had taken during the day. One picture of RB1 was particularly striking and he passed it around before zooming in and passing it around again. Their mouths fell open as each realised what he was focusing on.

Right in the centre of Rhino Bull 1's head was a bullet hole with a trace of blood around it. It had been almost impossible to make out with the naked eye. The effectiveness of the heavy duty armour plating that encased the rhino was amazing.

"This is what we are up against," Neil commented. "Fortunately for RB1, or Muto, as we have named him, it didn't penetrate and it almost seems to have bounced off. We were worried and so had the vet dart him, to sedate him and check him out, but all seems fine. He may not be as lucky next time..."

He left the words hanging for effect.

It was Harry who broke the silence.

"How could anyone be so barbaric to such amazing animals that aren't a threat to anyone? I just don't get it."

"You all have a lot to learn and our job is to try and educate you this week, so you will spread the message and not just be outraged, but actually do something about it. Our first priority on this project is to care for the rhinos and protect them in every way we can, but there are only six here. Somehow we need to let the world know what's happening and the tragedy and catastrophe that lie ahead if we don't re-educate the world about rhino horns, ivory and so many more endangered species. So get some rest, you're going to need it."

With that he made a dramatic exit, leaving them all intrigued.

RIP Chapter 16

Ted had spent the day resting and doodling, trying to get his first impressions of Africa down on paper, so he could paint when he got home.

Harry was too excited to sleep so had decided to browse through the library of wildlife books which the Reserve stocked. He was trying to find answers to some of the questions buzzing around his brain.

Rob and Tom went for a swim, but found the sun overpowering as it was now well over 40 degrees, so headed for the shade to listen to music and chill.

Tom had downloaded a song by Brad Cockcroft entitled 'Run Rhino Run!' which he played over and over. He liked the beat and had learnt the riffs on his Alvarez guitar, but the lyrics suddenly hit home like hammer blows after the morning's adventures.

"Guns and bullets and gangs and knives,
Money and blood and horns and lies.
Run rhino run!
Run away from the bullet and the gun."

The sad eyes of the rhinos they had seen pierced his soul and the words, "Rhinos can't fight back", reverberated around his head. He was determined to find answers to all his questions before heading home and sensed that in Neil and Christo he had an encyclopaedic knowledge which would help him do just that.

The afternoon game drive was as incredible as the first. The light was even more translucent, making the reds even redder and the sky a vivid blue, then red and then an orange which even painter Ted had never seen before.

Animals that had been sheltering from the heat and wallowing in waterholes appeared and seemed to accept the bakkie as one of them. The family tried to mentally keep a list of animals they had seen, but it was impossible. Zebras, giraffes, elephants, elands, kudus, impalas, nyalas, gemsboks, wildebeests, guinea fowl, ostriches...it was truly mind blowing.

As volunteers, they had tasks to do. Harry and Ted fixed a boundary fence which seemed to have been tampered with, Ellie, Rob and Tom cleared a pathway through the undergrowth where hazardous, spiky thorn bushes had taken over. It was definitely preferable to prune them with secateurs and loppers now, rather than catch them with their arms and heads later!

Labours complete, with sweat pouring from their brows, they hopped back on to the bakkie and drove back towards camp.

Tired but ecstatically content, they were ready for food and sleep, but Christo and Neil had yet another surprise in store. The vehicle took a sudden sharp right hand turn and headed up an extremely bumpy red track. They could feel their bones being well and truly shaken as they gripped the hand rail tightly for fear of being thrown off.

Just as suddenly the vehicle halted and Christo emerged from the cabin, carrying a large cooler bag.

"Follow me! The sun is about to set. We must get to the top of Venda 1 to toast the sundown and the stars."

Before anybody could reply, he headed off along the track to scale Venda 1 with a trail of bemused but willing disciples.

RIP Chapter 17

Venda 1 was a spectacular red stone escarpment which could be seen from all parts of the Reserve and was used as a reference point by the bakkie drivers. The path was difficult to follow at times, but Christo was their Sat Nav and he knew the route like the back of his hand.

The group followed Christo in a single file, creating a dust trail as they went, picking their way across boulders and scrambling up scree when necessary. Before they knew it, they were emerging around a shelf and found themselves on top of Venda 1 with a panoramic view of the Reserve.

Neil pointed out some fossils in the rock and told them about rock art and cave paintings which they would go and see later in the week, dating back thousands of years when the local Venda tribe lived there. He asked them to scour the mountain top for interesting rocks and fragments of pottery. Harry was his star pupil when he found a piece of earthenware, which had presumably been buried there for centuries.

The sun was setting on the horizon and the deep blue which they had enjoyed all day had faded and been replaced by a spectrum of reds and oranges, which had to be seen to be believed. Christo opened the cooler bag and passed round the bottles of Castle lager. They clinked bottles and raised them heavenward, repeating Christo's toast of 'Zivjeli'.

Stars were appearing everywhere and Tom couldn't resist bursting into song with his very own hearty rendition of Coldplay's 'A sky full of stars,' which he had heard hundreds of times, but could only now understand for the first time. It was yet another 'wow' moment on a day of so many and for once Ted was happy for his son to mark it in his own inimitable way.

They savoured the memory for some time until Christo announced:

"I'm sure you are hungry by now. It's time you experienced your first braai." With those cryptic words he led them back down the mountain and they headed back to the camp.

A 'braai', they discovered, was a traditional South African barbecue, but not like any they had ever had before. They were used to their dad's brave but lame efforts in their back garden. Invariably the food was rawer than when it had left the supermarket or even had the distinctive but gut-wrenching flavour of firelighters. Even more frequently, the British weather conspired to ruin the occasion and rather than 'al fresco' it became an 'in kitchen' meal.

The camp had its very own customised braai area which consisted of a fire pit in the ground with chairs and benches encircling it. There was a bar and grill area behind where the food and drink would be served.

The whole point of a braai, it transpired, was the

waiting and anticipation. The fire was lit using baobab or acacia wood, with no gas or firelighters in sight, and then it was a case of chatting and socialising while the 'slow food' was cooking. There was plenty of salad and bread to sustain you while you were waiting for the meat and fish to cook and there were endless bottles of Castle lager or Amarula, a local cream liqueur made from the fruit of the marula tree.

It was the perfect way to end a perfect day.

RIP Chapter 18

The food was the best that they had ever tasted. The steaks were succulent and full of natural flavour and the boerewors sausages were subtly spiced with hints of cloves, coriander and nutmeg. The food made your mouth water and your taste buds explode. Even the vegetarian option oozed flavour and was not just a meat and taste substitute - like they were at home.

It had taken a while for them all to unwind and relax, such had been the intensity of their experiences during their first day and the youngsters were used to "eating on the go" and fast food, so some adjustment of mind and stomach were required, but they all agreed that braais were THE best way to dine. The weather helped, of course, as it was still 30 degrees, Celsius not Fahrenheit, and there was an amazing array of stars with a full moon, to naturally light the proceedings.

Ted noticed, with interest, that all his sons were

comfortable and relaxed for a change, not checking their phones every couple of minutes or asking for the TV or music to be played.

Interestingly, Rob had clearly gravitated towards Neil and they were deep in conversation. Unusually, Rob was not making jokes or quoting statistics or even talking about football. He was listening intently. Ted wandered over and caught the end of Neil's story:

"So in my mid-twenties I'd had enough of the rat race in Ireland. I'd had a number of jobs which were all equally unfulfilling and was fed up with being lectured about the importance of holding down a steady job, so I could save to buy a house, meet a woman and start a family then live happily ever after. That wasn't for me and it was really playing with my head."

Ted understood why Rob was so fascinated. He was younger, but going through similar quandaries, having opted to get a job rather than go to university, but constantly feeling unsettled and disenchanted. For him, that was what this African adventure was all about.

"I decided to jack it all in and travel. Africa seemed exotic enough and distant enough, so I signed up for this project, not realising how it was going to turn me round and change my life. It took time. I was really homesick at first and packed several times to return home with my tail between my legs, like the Prodigal Son to beg forgiveness from my family, but something made me stay."

"We've only been here a day, but I can sense it already." It was definitely Rob's voice but it didn't sound like the words Rob would use.

Neil continued:

"I met Christo on a lion project and we hit it off immediately and became good friends. When that project ended we went our separate ways, but vowed to work on a conservation project together as soon as one came up. So when Howard wanted protection and monitoring of his rhinos, we became Mutogomeli or guardians. Since then, dozens of volunteers, just like your family and Ellie have brought their baggage, physical and emotional, to join us to 'observe, research, understand, plan and change', as our motto puts it."

RIP Chapter 19

The braai was in full swing, with food and drink freely flowing with animated conversation. Ted had joined Neil and Rob's discussion, intrigued by some of the detail.

Neil had explained how the Mutogomeli idea had been born, blossomed and flourished and as an ex-teacher himself, he was particularly interested in the education aspect.

"Would you describe yourself as a conservationist or teacher?" he asked.

"Undoubtedly both, as I am paid to protect Howard's rhinos, but I am also in charge of the volunteers, so I look after their safety and well-being and try and make their stay as special and memorable as possible, but even more importantly empower them to return home and educate others. We have had visitors from all over the world and some go home to raise money to support us, but that's a drop in the ocean. We need a change of mind set, particularly in China and the Far East where rhino horn is so coveted."

Ted had read about the demand for rhino horn which was touted as a cure for cancer and hangovers - being sold on the black market at prices equivalent to gold, diamonds and cocaine. Poaching had increased by 8000% since 2007 due to the high demand and that showed no sign of declining.

"It's so frustrating. You saw those beautiful, vulnerable animals and that's only six. We can make a difference here, but that's only the tip of a huge iceberg. From one dead end job to another, I have finally found a purpose, a mission, a driving force, a reason for living. I came out here to run away from responsibility, society, even myself and ended up finding much, much more. I hope and pray, young Rob, that the same thing happens to you..."

Ted echoed the words and sentiment in his head and his heart. His middle son was a complex character.

He had always been active, loved his sport and was the joker in the pack, but his dad knew this was a cover-up and merely a facade that he portrayed to the world as a coping mechanism.

School had been a challenge for him as he lacked focus and tended to drift along, which had been fine up to the memory test that was GCSEs, but A Levels demanded more application and focus and that wasn't really Rob.

Getting a job to earn pocket money so he could play and watch sport in every leisure moment satisfied Rob in his late teens and early twenties, but then mum died and his whole world imploded overnight. He had been the angry one; while Harry busied himself with projects and Tom asked endless, unanswerable questions and his dad fell apart at the seams.

This trip was time for all of them to take stock and even after one day, he could sense a change. He had found a kindred spirit in Neil and was determined to spend as much time as possible with him in the hope that by understanding him, he may just begin to understand himself.

A glance at his watch made Ted jump. Surely it couldn't be 11 o'clock already?

"I'm off to Bedfordshire," he declared. "And I expect you all up with the sweet silver song of the lark at 4am, not 4pm, Tom. Sweet dreams."

RIP Chapter 20

Ted ambled into the kitchen and rubbed his eyes in disbelief. It was 4am and still dark and yet there in front of him, bright eyed and bushy tailed, were his three sons tucking into their breakfasts and chatting excitedly about the day ahead.

"Good morning! No need for the woodpecker today." He smiled and all three lads cringed at the memory of cold winter school mornings when the only way to rouse reluctant teenagers was for their dad to drum on their heads with his forefinger whispering:

"Woody says it's time to rise and shine." It was never the best way to start the day.

Neil and Christo were busy dealing with finances and paperwork, so Jason, a young Australian intern was to be their driver and guide. Rob was a little disappointed. He had been looking forward to picking Neil's brains again, but there was plenty of time for that and braais were a better forum.

They filled their water bottles with the limestone tasting tap water and topped it up with ice from the freezer. Even now the temperature was well into the thirties and a scorcher was predicted. It was Africa after all.

Ellie had decided to give the morning drive a miss so she could help Christo and Neil sort out provisions for the rest of the week.

Ted rode up front in the bakkie cabin with Jason and Harry, which meant that Rob and Tom had the back to themselves, or so they thought...

"Can you guys sit on the front bench please? We're picking up three extra passengers at the main camp and they can huddle together on the back row."

Harry wondered why Jason used the word "huddle" when there was room for four adults but decided not to ask as he couldn't wait to get going and experience the wonders of the Bush for a second time.

Jason checked out the bakkie, pumped up the front tyre which apparently had a slow puncture (not the most reassuring news when you are heading out into the land of leopards, lions and buffaloes who saw you as an exotic lunch) and loaded two bales of hay for the rhinos' breakfast. Then they were off on their third drive.

It was a stunning morning and the sun was just rising to illuminate the track as they drove towards the main camp. Ted hopped out to open the main gate and they pulled into a clearing next to an impressive mansion with a sparkling outdoor swimming pool and two more rondavels, similar to their sleeping quarters, but somewhat grander and more luxurious.

Jason disappeared around the back while Ted and the boys waited patiently, wondering who was going to join them. As always they couldn't resist making it into a game.

Ted guessed first:

"I reckon it will be three Americans in their eighties in full safari gear. Here to tick one off their bucket lists." Rob was next.

"I think it will be three famous footballers on their summer break, maybe Lion Massai, Rhinoldinho and Rhinaldo."

They all groaned at the puns and wondered how long he had been thinking them up.

"I guess it will be two journalists and David Attenborough researching a BBC documentary."

Harry as always wanted to win, so he waited until they had all declared and more importantly, until he had seen who was on the way with Jason.

"You're all wrong as usual. It'll be three ripped actors in full American army uniform, making a film."

RIP Chapter 21

The extra passengers were indeed American, they were certainly muscular and they were wearing full military combat gear, but they weren't actors.

"Hi. I'm Shane and my two buddies are Ryan and Joe. We're from Vetpaw and we're gonna join you this morning if that's OK with you?"

They weren't about to argue. All three of them towered above everybody else, well over six feet tall and about six feet wide too. They were indeed in full camouflage combat gear, but the material barely held their rippling muscles and it seemed that at any moment they may burst out of their clothes, like the Incredible Hulk.

Shane had his sleeves rolled up, revealing a row of tattoos and insignia which Tom made a mental note to ask about, when he could summon up the courage.

Ted introduced his sons and they all shook hands, trying desperately to match the bone crushing grip of the newcomers.

"You can tell a lot from a handshake. First impressions at an interview are crucial," Harry remembered being told. "Too limp and you come across as weak and indecisive. Too firm and you run the risk of seeming aggressive and too forceful."

But nobody would dare tell any of these guys that their handshake was dodgy. They would definitely get the job!

Jason and Ted climbed back into the cabin; Harry, Rob and Tom took the front pew and Shane, Ryan and Joe huddled together and overhung the side of the bakkie...

As they headed off to seek out, their precious protégés, nobody spoke. The scenery was too beautiful, the wildlife too amazing and the company too intimidating. Rob nudged Tom and gestured towards their co-travellers and in particular their waists. They all had military rifles slung over their shoulders and as a backup wore holsters complete with scary looking hand guns "Unusual for vets," Rob thought. "It must be a Tasers and dart guns."

Ted had decided to take some photographs to help him with his art work when he got home, so Jason stopped the vehicle frequently to allow him to capture bouncy impalas, impressive elands, iconic zebras and elephants as well as countless others.

Harry enjoyed pointing them out to the Americans, feeling an expert regurgitating the snippets of information which Neil had shared the day before.

The giraffes were Tom's favourites. He had seen them in the zoo and been fascinated by them, but seeing them in the wild was another level. They were over 18 feet high and Tom was struck by the upstanding mane on their long necks, their steeply sloping shoulders and their expressive, soulful eyes. Their tongues were incredibly long and their horns were covered in light skin. Their bodies were an intricate tapestry with blotches of lighter hair making patterns, which he had read were unique in each animal and made them easy to identify.

The two characteristics Tom loved the most were their habit of staring and the way they ran like elongated rabbits. Their long legs working in pairs to reach a top speed of 37 miles per hour.

It was almost impossible for a giraffe to hide. Their heads peeped out over the tallest trees. They would have won the wooden spoon in an Animal 'Hide-and-Seek' Olympics. Their answer to potential predators was to just stare them out!

Tom tried to outstare Lofty, as he called the male with the extra horn and darker spots. He failed miserably. He couldn't help but laugh out loud and wonder at God's sense of humour.

RIP Chapter 22

The rhinos were less elusive on Day 2 and they were still in two groups of three in the same area as the previous day. Jason tracked them with ease and fed them with the fresh hay. He seemed to have a real bond with them, though he was quick to explain that they were truly wild animals. It was vital that they didn't become too comfortable in human company or too dependent. This would render the rhinos helpless if poachers came on the scene.

The Americans were fascinated by the proceedings and conversed in whispers behind their hands, almost as if they were used to being recorded and overheard. Tom's head was spinning with questions, but he too was enjoying the experience and decided to leave his interrogation until a more suitable occasion.

They dropped the Americans off on their way back to camp and Tom was delighted to hear Jason invite them over for a braai that evening. That would be his chance. They all high-fived, low-fived and fist-pumped and laughed when Ted insisted on a traditional British handshake - only to pull his hand away at the last moment.

Back at camp, Neil, Ellie and Christo had gone off to Polokwane to do the weekly shop and chores so Ted and family hungrily devoured their second breakfasts of the day and all opted for a return to bed to shelter from the sun and get some shut-eye so as to be ready for the afternoon drive and evening braai.

As there were no specific tasks to do, Jason decided that the sundowners' drive would be an elephant tracker, as he wanted to take some photos for his blog. As always they saw some amazing sights on their way to Venda 1, including huge millipedes and scarily monstrous myriad spiders.

They scaled the mountain and scanned the horizon for elephant activity. A herd of buffaloes were roaming in the far distance and they also spotted unmistakable giraffes and a group of baboons heading up a nearby cliff, but no elephants. It was inconceivable that a herd of such huge animals could hide so completely, but apparently that was the norm.

They headed back to the bakkie and drove to the mine dumps. These were impressive in themselves.

Limestone had been quarried hundreds of years ago and huge mounds or dumps had been formed which gave the area an almost eerily moonscape feel. It was like the loose scree that they had encountered in Snowdonia the previous summer. It was hard work on the calf and thigh muscles, but they all managed to scramble up in Jason's wake.

Again they scanned the horizon, this time with success. A group of about a dozen elephants were down by the southern fence, a couple of miles away.

Jason was off like a greyhound, sliding and jumping down the scree slope. He was in the vehicle almost before everyone else had set off. Once everyone was boarded, the bakkie set off, in hot Jumbo pursuit.

RIP Chapter 23

The elephants proved even more elusive than the rhinos. Jason managed to pick up their tracks, but they were clearly moving at great speed. Elephants had the advantage of being able to crash through the Bush undergrowth, rather than follow the few roads that the bakkie was forced to take.

The devastation caused by the elephants was striking. Ted and the boys realised why farmers and landowners discouraged elephants from their farms and Reserves. Nothing survived in their wake and they seemed to enjoy destroying shrubbery, crops and trees - just because they could.

Eventually, after what seemed an age, Jason slowed the bakkie to a crawl and pointed out of the window. There, on the hill above them, a herd of a dozen elephants were grazing and feeding. They were truly impressive beasts, larger than you imagined. A definite threat in the wild, where there were no fences to protect the onlooker.

One particularly awesome female elephant was at the front of the group and was clearly the leader or matriarch. The bakkie was far enough away not to have raised an alarm, but she was nonetheless lifting her trunk and testing the air.

One signal from this female elephant and the herd would be gone. Hopefully they would choose flight rather than fight. The bakkie would be futile, as protection, should the herd decide to charge.

Jason and Ted were busily clicking away with their cameras and the boys watched wonderstruck until suddenly the matriarch curled her trunk in the air and charged off into the undergrowth. She was followed, dutifully, by the rest of the herd.

The viewing had been relatively brief, but had nonetheless made a lasting impression on all of them. Whereas the rhinos looked somewhat haunted and sorrowful, the elephants were positively threatening and aggressive. The bakkie passengers were all disappointed and yet, at the same time, relieved that the elephants had gone.

Time had passed incredibly quickly. The huge African sun was sinking fast. It was time to head for the nearest peak. In this case it was the mine dumps. The group were ready to toast the sunset with a sundowners' tipple.

They scrambled gamely back up the scree slope and reached the top just in time to see another truly stunning African sunset. The sky turning from a warm golden glow, through reds and oranges, almost like a vast celestial bush fire.

The only sounds were of wildlife, with hyenas and baboons calling to one another, but other than that it was perfect, complete peace. Even the Castle lager tasted different, somehow the flavour was more intense and the coldness really attacked their senses as it trickled down.

It was almost as if the earth itself was sighing

contentedly at the beauty of the evening and the spectacular light show. One by one, stars began to appear. They were distinguishable for a while, until the numbers grew and grew. The vast amount of stars seemed to almost merge into one another.

Reluctantly the stargazers dragged themselves away and headed for home. Jason put Tom on spotlight duty. His job was to scan the trees and bushes along the track, on the lookout for leopards or predators. Fortunately, none were out and about. Rob felt compelled to finish the trip with one of his random jokes.

"Why are leopards useless at hide and seek? ...because they are always spotted." Everybody groaned, but Rob knew that Miss Pender, his registration teacher who favoured leopard print fashion, would have approved.

RIP Chapter 24

Christo, Neil and Ellie had returned and been busy setting up the fire for the braai, so evening meal was nearly ready. Venison steaks were tonight's special treat, but there were also plenty of alternatives, with pasta dishes, fish and spicy sausages to tempt all palates.

The Vetpaw soldiers were the guests of honour. They had clearly been enjoying liquid hospitality for some time, judging by the recycling box, which was already bulging with empty red wine and beer bottles.

Ted chatted with Christo and Neil, quizzing them about the elephants, intrigued by the fact that the rhinos on the Reserve were endangered and at high risk for their horns and yet the herd of elephants they had seen, with their impressive tusks, seemed relatively safe in spite of the potential ivory market.

Christo explained:

"It's all about supply and demand. Rhino horn is currently like gold dust. Ivory is still popular, but the market has been flooded and the customer base is relatively limited. It has a durable quality and an aesthetic appeal and was historically used to make the whites of eyes for statues. Before plastic was invented, ivory was used to make cutlery handles, musical instruments, billiard balls and piano keys. Unfortunately, the song is wrong. Ebony and ivory can't really live together in perfect harmony, at least not for the poor elephants."

Ted wished that the boys were listening. This was real education, proper opening of minds.

"The demand for ivory is therefore more finite. Rhino horn is mostly sold as powder as a medicine or designer drug, so demand is growing and tragically infinite. The only hope we have is to educate the potential customer with the facts about the dangers of extinction, but more importantly the lack of scientific evidence to back up wild theories about rhino horn curing cancer. The horn is made from keratin, so you are just as likely to be cured of cancer by doing this..."

He stopped speaking and chewed one of his finger nails.

"Finger nails are made of exactly the same material. So save up all your finger and toe nail clippings and post them off to China or Vietnam. Flood the market, make them realise how ridiculous it is and you might save a species."

It was clearly hyperbole, but an interesting argument.

Ted glanced around and was surprised and delighted to see his three sons in deep conversation with the American soldiers. He excused himself and wandered over to listen in on their debate.

As usual, Tom was asking all the questions and Ryan, Shane and Joe were doing their best to satisfy his curiosity.

"So you aren't vets at all."

"No, Vetpaw is an acronym for Veterans Empowered to Protect African Wildlife. We all served in the Special Forces group in Iraq, Afghanistan and Syria, seeing plenty of action."

Ted knew that Tom would interrupt and was not to be disappointed.

"What sort of action?"

Ted was not expecting an answer, but this time was wrong.

"We are trained soldiers, the elite, and the best in the world. Our mission was to take out Saddam Hussein. We were successful. Our mission was to free Afghanistan from the threat of the Taliban after 9/11. We were successful. Our mission was to support the Free Syrian Army in its fight against ISIS. We were successful."

Ted was struck by the simplicity, yet complexity, of Joe's words, but even more struck by Tom's next bombshell.

RIP Chapter 25

"Do you feel that you left Iraq, Afghanistan and Syria in a better or a worse state than when you intervened?"

It was the six million dollar question and Ted could almost sense the tension and anticipation in the air between his pacifist sons and professional war machines. But Joe's answer threw him completely.

"Listen. We come from very different backgrounds and experiences. I'm guessing that with a teacher dad and university education, you've got your own stories to tell."

Rob shuffled his feet but said nothing.

"I dropped out of school early and signed up to join the army at 17. I was drifting and in danger of losing direction completely. A lot of my buddies got heavily into drugs or booze or both..."

He gazed into the distance, deep in thought.

"I wanted to do something with my life and fighting for my country against the forces of evil in the world was my way out, my way forward. The training was rigorous and I dedicated myself to becoming the strongest, fastest, bravest soldier I could be. I cannot tell you how special and proud I felt when I was chosen for the Special Forces group and given my first green beret. My self-esteem which had been at rock bottom, was now up with the stars. Our motto is: 'De oppresso libero'. No doubt you geeks know what that means?"

Harry couldn't resist showing off his Latin GCSE knowledge, in spite of the jibe.

"Is it 'To free the oppressed'?"

"So that was our mission. To free Iraq from Saddam Hussein, to free the Afghanistan and Syrian people from oppression and most importantly free the whole world from the threat of terrorist groups like the Taliban and ISIS. Did we succeed? Undoubtedly yes. Did we leave the three countries in a better or worse state? That will be for history to judge. But surely it would have been worse not to have tried. Burke said: 'The only thing necessary for the triumph of evil is for good men to do nothing.'"

Ted found it strange to hear such a famous quote being used in this context, but it certainly drilled home the point.

Joe continued:

"At 30 we are forced to retire from service and, after what we have seen and experienced, it's hard. Some find it impossible. So rather than going home to be a barman in Boston, I am here to help the oppressed of Kuduland, the rhinos. I was programmed to destroy evil. Now I am programmed to use the same skills to protect. This is a different kind of war, but poachers use guns and machetes as weapons, so we must respond accordingly."

They had all read about the Ivory War and Rhino Horn Wars, but somehow it had all just become more of a reality.

"They have beaten the poachers in Kaziranga in India by shooting fifty poachers in the last three years. It's funny how that got the message across. If we need to do that here..."

Ted had to interject.

"But the beauty of this place is the peace, the calm, the oneness with nature. Surely making it a war zone will destroy all that."

"So good men like you, say 'do nothing' and before you know it there are no rhinos and no elephants to come and see in the wild. We are not the bad guys. The poachers are. We are here to protect, not provoke. This is a deterrent, not a threat."

He pointed to the holster and his hand gun.

"And are you prepared to die for the rhinos, like you were for your country?"

"Absolutely, we all regrettably survived Iraq, Afghanistan and Syria, but there is still hope of Valhalla if we die in the Bush of South Africa."

RIP Chapter 26

The boys had all heard of Valhalla as it had been mentioned in their GCSE Religious Studies course as the Norse equivalent of heaven. They never expected to meet anyone who believed it to be the location for the afterlife and were really excited at the prospect.

Ted and family had been through great soul-searching and doubt since the tragic and traumatic death of Rosie, their beloved wife and mum, two years before. They all wanted to believe that she was now free of the terrible suffering she had endured and had gone to a happy resting place. As Christians, they hoped and prayed that this was heaven, rather than death leading to re-incarnation or being the end as other religions believed. As a family they had agonised with the different possibilities and debated them long into the night when the initial shock and all-consuming grief had dulled. But Valhalla had never even been considered and they were all fascinated to learn more.

"As fighting men, warriors, we all hope to die in battle rather than a prolonged, drawn out agony of retirement and old age."

It was mind blowing for all of them to hear 30 year olds as incredibly physically fit and strong as these soldiers moaning about retirement, but that was their life. Ted had agonised about retiring at the relatively youthful age of 57 and was still unsure, but thirty?

"It obviously doesn't apply to you guys, but we all hope to go in a glorious blaze of glory so that Odin will select us to fight in his eternal battle in his golden halls."

There was a moment's stunned silence while the others tried to take in his words. Tom was the first to respond.

"What happens if you don't die in battle or aren't selected? What about the rest of us? Where are my mum, nan and grandad now?"

Ted glanced at him and thought about rebuking him about the directness and almost hostility in his tone, but decided against it. After all, it was exactly what they were all wondering.

"Half of those who die in battle and are not chosen by Odin are selected by Freya to keep the women who died as maiden's company. Not too bad..."

Harry and Rob smiled, while Tom looked a bit embarrassed.

"A bit like a Norse Tinder," Rob joked.

Ted moved them on quickly to avoid another man-to-man chat with Tom which he always dreaded.

"What about the others - the sick and elderly - who die of illness or natural causes?"

"They go to a foggy realm to share the afterlife with the goddess Hel."

"Sounds like a choice between hell and Hel," mused Rob.

"It might seem like hell to you, but it's paradise for us. What's your alternative? Live a 'good life' and be rewarded with harps and hymns and a chance to worship God forever."

Ted interrupted again.

"That's not quite what the Bible says."

"OK then. There will be a new heaven and a new earth, a Holy City, a New Jerusalem and God will wipe every tear away and there will be no more dying, suffering or crying and a new order will be established. That's what Revelation says."

It was strange to hear a Valhalla believer quoting the bible, but he clearly had done his study and knew his stuff.

"So life is all about choices and I choose Valhalla.

Nobody actually knows. It's all about faith. My life is dedicated to fighting for good against evil, just as you would say that you try to do good deeds rather than bad, so that's what I hope and pray I will be doing for eternity."

He was interrupted by Christo.

"Grub's up! Goeie gesondheid en n Lang lewe. That's Afrikaans for good health and long life."

The phrase was never more appropriate.

RIP Chapter 27

Ted hadn't slept well. He had dreamt of hiding behind a massive, ornate, bejewelled, golden throne with the name Odin emblazoned on it, while battle raged all around and armoured warriors fought endlessly with every weapon they could get their hands on. They were all laughing and smiling, but he was too terrified to come out from his safe haven and guessed that he would be there forever. The braai had been delicious as always and the lager had flown freely, so much so that they had only made it to bed around midnight. He was therefore impressed to see all three of his sons stirring and getting up without complaint at silly o'clock.

The debate had been intense the night before and he couldn't wait to get his sons alone to see their reactions and develop it further.

They grabbed a swift breakfast and boarded the bakkie.

Neil was driving and tracking, so they were looking forward to an informative, educational and entertaining morning under African skies.

"If you guys don't mind jumping on the back, we've got a passenger to pick up on the way out. I'll have to be on my best behaviour for once. It's someone related to Howard the boss. It's Howard's son Gavin. If you think I'm an expert, wait until you get talking to Gav. He's had 14 years study."

Ted and his sons were intrigued and excited at the prospect.

As the bakkie pulled away, Ted was determined to take his opportunity.

"So what did you think of Action Man and company last night?"

Rob held his head in his hands.

"They blew my poor, little brain. I hate it when people mess with my head."

Harry was more philosophical.

"I thought they were fascinating to talk to. They've had such different lives to us and yet I felt a real bond and kinship. It did make me think about priorities and how we are brainwashed into believing that education, education, education is the key to success and happiness."

Ted might have expected this from Rob, but coming from the lips of his oldest and most academic son, it came as a bit of a shock.

"Don't you think they are brainwashed too, with all this 'mission' business?"

Harry's reply was immediate.

"Our mission is set by society, our parents and our schools. Work hard at school and you will get the qualifications necessary to get a good job and that in turn will ensure you have enough money to buy a house, pay the bills and live happily ever after."

Ted thought back to his own youth and recognised the pattern. It was a day when there were no tuition fees and he had even received a grant and sponsorship to go to university.

"The Tories, thankfully, changed all that," he said sarcastically. "There are hardly any jobs for graduates. Also you have huge debts to start your working life. That certainly makes you think twice and re-prioritise." He glanced at Rob who was nodding and Tom who was deep in thought.

"But would you swap your upbringing and school years for Joe's or Ryan's life - from what we heard last night? What about their future and your future? And then there's Valhalla..."

Before there was time to answer, the bakkie pulled up near the Lodge and a smiling Gavin bounded on board.

RIP Chapter 28

Gavin introduced himself and high fived the lads and shook Ted's hand vigorously and enthusiastically. Ted was wracking his brain as to why he looked so familiar. He looked vaguely like his nephew Dan, with a shock of blonde hair and an ever-present grin, but it was more than that. Suddenly he remembered where he had seen him before. He had read an article in Fieldsports Magazine which had really made him think.

Gavin had grown up in the Bush - so his upbringing couldn't be more different to Harry, Rob and Tom. He could drive a Land Cruiser, track animals through seemingly impenetrable undergrowth, fish, hunt and ride horses. He had kept three lions, a leopard, a nyala, a warthog and a huge black Rhodesian Ridgeback dog, called Bear, as pets and all before his fourteenth birthday. As the son of the Reserve landowner that was not surprising, but Ted had found the Fieldsports Magazine article fascinating and shared it with the family one teatime.

Gavin proved to be another superb guide, pointing out tracks as they drove along. He entertained with tales of growing up in the Bush. There were stories of close shaves with scorpions, leopards, buffaloes and snakes.

Gavin helped Neil with the telemetry and they tracked down the rhinos with a minimum of fuss, which demonstrated clearly their expertise and knowledge.

The rhinos seemed happy and healthy. It was almost impossible to believe that in such idyllic surroundings they were the centre of such a violent and intense battle, which was escalating so rapidly that the cavalry, in this case US Special Forces, had been called in. The soulful, haunted expression of the rhinos made more sense now.

Gavin pointed out sausage trees and poisonous Spirostachys trees with their deadly latex. Local tribesmen still used it on their arrow tips when hunting. He had stories about armies of soldier ants and humongous myriad spiders which enthralled them. Gavin knew his way around the dense bush so instinctively that he had earned the nickname 'Sat Gav'.

Back at camp, Ted opted for rest. Tom and Rob were reluctant to do the same, choosing instead to play cricket with Gavin, in the shade of the baobab. The cricketers later cooled off in the outdoor pool.

Ted knew that the boys would regret not resting later, but it was all part of the adventure. Ted had really warmed to Gavin, discovering him to be a highly intelligent, sociable young man, who seemed older than his fourteen years. He was nothing like the hunting, killing machine that the magazine article had painted.

Ted made a mental note to discuss bias and the manipulative nature of the media with Tom. Ted's youngest son, Tom, was hoping to train as a journalist at the first possible opportunity.

Gavin came with the adventurers again on the sundowners' drive. He helped Neil give a complete guided tour of the property. They were focusing on checking the boundary fences, which were vital for keeping intruders out.

Ted was delighted to see his sons laughing and joking again, while toasting the sunset. The trip to Africa had been a high risk option. It was, however, proving to be a roaring success. Though it was a confused picture when it came to protecting the rhinos and it was about to become even more complicated at that evening's braai when Ted met Howard, Gavin's dad.

RIP Chapter 29

Ted had only really encountered South Africans on the rugby or cricket field, but Howard was the embodiment of his characteristic South African male. He was dressed in a khaki safari shirt and knee length shorts and he had the warmest, sunniest smile which seemed to reflect the African climate and hospitality.

Rob and Tom were happily chatting with Gavin about the day's events and Christo, Neil and Ellie were busy preparing the braai and accompaniments, so Harry and Ted were able to quiz Howard and find out more about the project and the plight of the rhinos.

"So what do you think of Kuduland and the ranch?" Ted was surprised at the use of the word "ranch", as in his head it conjured up pictures of 'The High Chaparral' where cattle and sheep were raised and bred for meat and wool. How did this fit with a wildlife conservation project and the rhinos? He was about to find out.

"We all really love the wildlife and scenery and everybody has been so friendly and welcoming. Gavin told us earlier that it's a family project and has been going for over forty years."

"That's right. My dad started it up in 1974 and we now have more than 8000 animals, including our six precious rhinos. We love to share it with visitors who come to view, photograph and hunt, though our main income is from the annual game sale. This year we broke all records selling a Blue ostrich for 30,000 rand, a kudu Bull for 60,000 rand and a waterbuck bull for a whopping 75,000 rand."

Harry looked visibly shaken by the word "hunt" and the thought of the beautiful animals that they had seen roaming free, being sold and presumably slaughtered for meat.

Howard sensed his discomfort.

"Sorry man. Are you a vegetarian?"

Ted replied on his son's behalf.

"No. It's just a confusing idea for us. We live in a different world where meat comes from Tesco or Marks and Spencer, if you're earning enough. I always tell the lads that if you had to go out and kill your dinner rather than buy it pre-packed, we'd all be veggies."

"Nonsense! Have you tasted the braai steaks?"

He had a point. The steaks and boerewors sausages were truly scrumptious.

"That money will pay the bills including Gavin's school fees, and may enable us to buy more rhinos, possibly black ones too, if we can get clearance. Hopefully the Vetpaw guys you met yesterday will help us to achieve that. So breeding and selling three animals and allowing tourists to hunt others could help to save a species from extinction."

Harry was confused. It didn't take much. One of his teachers, Mrs Williams, had tried to explain a farmer's wife's perspective to him, but without success.

"But how can anyone enjoy hunting defenceless animals?"

Ted felt his hand gripping the lager bottle tighter. Howard was a personable, charismatic character but looked like he worked out regularly and could clearly handle a gun, so not one to antagonise. But he simply smiled and continued amiably.

"Look. We are all on the same side. We all want to save the rhinos, and elephants and other endangered species for that matter, it's just we have different views and varying means to achieve the same end. That's why we started the volunteer project in the first place. We want you to leave here educated about the problem and enthused to do something about it, but if you were expecting easy solutions or even one cure-all you are going to be disappointed. Let's grab some food and another beer. I'll give you the facts and let you make up your own minds."

RIP Chapter 30

Ted had discussed post-truth with friends and colleagues, deciding that it could be particularly useful when the HMI inspectors called, if you could tell them, "My facts are not your facts." He believed that anybody was entitled to their own opinions, but not to their own facts.

Howard had some facts for Ted.

"Rhinos are being poached. In the Vhembe district there are 8 reserves and all their rhinos have been killed. I personally have lost four in the last two years and my next door neighbour lost four in a week last October. That's not scaremongering. I can show you the pictures of the dismembered corpses on my phone if it helps."

Howard reached for his pocket, but Ted waved him away.

"South Africa relies on tourists for income and jobs, but I can show you emails from visitors who vow never to return. They also deter others from coming. Their motivation was to come for the 'tranquillity and peace' but described it as a 'war zone'. Other families on a game drive came across a freshly poached rhino and were so traumatised that they took the next plane home."

"So what is the answer?" Ted enquired.

"I've given you my facts and I'm sure Christo and Neil have given you plenty more. Now my opinion. It's threefold. First, our government must clamp down on captured poachers and give longer jail sentences to deter others. Secondly, conservationists like us need more support and positive press. The Vetpaw guys may well be part of that. Thirdly, and most importantly, the people who buy rhino horn need educating. It's a fact that it can't cure cancer. It's a fact that if they keep on buying Ivory and rhino horn, their numbers will diminish, dwindle, and they may even become extinct."

Ted and Harry agreed with all three of the points, but wondered exactly how they could be achieved.

Lobbying a supposedly corrupt government seemed futile; turning Reserves into war zones would possibly deter would-be poachers but in the meantime would always be likely to deter would-be visitors. Educating the Chinese and Vietnamese about these issues could be very difficult. The mind boggles.

The whole hunting aspect needed clarification for Harry. Howard was such a caring, articulate and nature-loving character, that it was difficult to imagine him wielding a rifle and leading trophy hunting adrenaline junkies into the Bush, returning with a bloodstained carcass.

"I see how farming works, but how can you excuse hunting? Surely you don't condone or enjoy that side of your ranch?"

Again, Howard's expression never changed.

"It costs thousands of pounds every year to feed and protect the rhinos and that's where my profits go. I don't expect you to understand or support hunting. You live in a completely different world. I bet you even tell your cat off if it kills a bird or mouse."

Ted and Harry shared a knowing smile. Harry had sat lecturing Nelson several times about becoming a vegi-cat or at least just surviving on Felix instead of hunting and capturing cute baby goldfinches.

"I thought so, it is nature. Watch a David Attenborough documentary and you'll see what I mean. There are more killings in those than any psycho-murder film. I grew up watching a real life version, witnessing cute impalas and impressive nyalas being stalked and hunted down by lions and leopards. It was never a fair fight. You knew the outcome, but it was still hypnotic to watch. I guess that's why it's in my blood. So if some rich American wants to pay silly money to hunt and shoot one of my antelope, or even one of my giraffes, then as long as it's a fair chase on foot, then I'll take their money and buy some more rhinos."

None of it made sense to Harry, but one word stood out.

RIP Chapter 31

"Did you say giraffe?" Harry could scarcely believe his ears. The giraffes had quickly become his favourite sighting and the thought of one being gunned down, horrified him.

"In the last twenty years, five giraffes have been hunted. We choose them carefully and with considerable heart-searching. If they are suffering or too old to cope in the wild, I'd rather earn thousands of rand having them hunted and shot, rather than watch them slowly die. Don't tell me you don't believe in having animals put to sleep when they are old or in pain? And the revenue it brings in pays for the conservation and protection of the rhinos and elephants which are being hunted illegally and indiscriminately and suffering horribly."

Ted thought of Boris and Bruce; family pets that had been much loved, but had to be put to sleep when their health deteriorated.

Harry's face spoke volumes about his distaste at what he had heard.

Howard continued:

"I don't expect you to agree with our methods or modus operandi, but these are the facts and I will leave you to make your own mind up. There were only two game ranches when we started ours in the 1970s, whereas today there are over six hundred. It is the fastest growing sector of the agricultural economy in South Africa and many cattle farmers are becoming game ranchers and undergoing training, just as I did in Texas. This brings in thousands of pounds, dollars and Euros which can either make the rancher rich, or, in my case, be used to buy, feed and conserve rhinos and elephants to save them from extinction."

It was a strong argument, but Harry was far from convinced.

"But there must be another way."

"If you find one, please let me know. I've heard countless conservationists make passionate, emotional speeches on 'Save the rhino' or 'Protect the elephant', but it's always about raising money and keeping them safe in zoos or feeding them in the wild. That's a bottomless pit I'm afraid and in the meantime numbers are dwindling. The do-gooders mean well, but it needs action as well as words."

Ted and family had discussed Foreign Aid a number of times when Red Nose Day or Children in Need came around and he knew how seemingly straightforward, but actually complicated the arguments were when it came to short-term solutions, dependency, corruption and ensuring that it got through to the needy and desperate, rather than being consumed by administration charges or overheads.

"What we do here, as you have already discovered, is different to other projects. We offer hunts, but also photographic safaris and educational trips like yours. Our mission is to share this wonderful part of the world and these awesome animals with guests from other countries, firstly to raise money to fund it, but more importantly to make you aware, make you think and ultimately, when you return home, galvanise you to inform others and act. Our motto is 'Observe, Research, Understand, Plan, and Change.' The first three are down to us. The last two are up to you."

Ted had hoped and prayed when planning the holiday that it would be exciting and life-changing for all four of them and at the end of day three was convinced that it had already exceeded expectations and would continue to do so.

RIP Chapter 32

Four a.m. had become everybody's favourite time of day. There was something about being up at sunrise which was exhilarating and enriching. It made you feel more alive than ever, once you'd silenced the dreaded alarm and convinced your body to rise and shine.

It had been after midnight when they had retired; Rob and Tom saying a reluctant good night to their new best friend Gavin, with Ted and Harry warmly shaking Howard by the hand, thanking him for his hospitality and stimulating conversation.

The Americans joined the family on the morning drive and everybody was in high spirits. Their uncertainty and alarm, at being accompanied by armed Norse warriors or Berserkers, as they had nicknamed them, had dissipated after getting to know them properly at the braai. The family realised what fascinating, fun-loving characters they were.

Rob was on good form, asking them to teach them an army cadence marching chant. Ted knew he was up to something, but wasn't sure what.

Joe was as friendly and obliging as ever.

"The chorus for you to join in is:

'Mama, mama, can't you see,
What the army's done for me?'"

Joe, Ryan and Shane started them off.

"Mama, mama, can't you see
What the army's done for me?
They put me in a barber's chair,
Spun me round, I had no hair.

"Altogether!
Mama, mama, can't you see
What the army's done for me?
They took away my favourite jeans,

Now I'm wearing army greens."

The lyrics were amusing, but as the boys joined in, they couldn't help musing that this would have been used as a battle cry in the war zones of Iraq, Afghanistan and Syria.

When they had finished, Rob chipped in:

"If you are going to be here for a while and be accompanying British tourists, you should learn a British Army version."

Ted gave Rob his withering dad's look, dreading what was coming. He expected 'You'll never walk alone' or 'Ring of Fire', but it was neither.

"This, historically, is the most common to be used by British soldiers. I think it was written by Winston Churchill himself."

The Americans looked suitably impressed.

"The chorus is 'All day long.' I'll start us off. I'll change it slightly to make it more relevant to the Bush."

He then chanted with a totally straight face:

"The wheels on the bakkie go
round and round,
round and round,
round and round,
The wheels on the bakkie go
round and round
all day long."

Ted had to pinch himself that he wasn't dreaming or hallucinating as he heard the soldiers belt out the chorus after hearing that the wipers were swishing, the doors opening and shutting, the horn beeping, the gas glugging, money clinking and rangers shushing. He sensed that this would be Rob's legacy and wondered how many British tourists would play along, before some pedant ruined it by telling them the true history of the traditional nursery rhyme.

Rob wasn't finished. His most mischievous smile was on show.

"Before we get to the rhinos, we wondered if you could do us a favour."

Ted winced. He had experienced Rob's 'favours' before.

"My dad used to be a teacher and the kids had lots of look-alike nicknames for him. You may not have heard of Arsene Wenger or Mr. Bean, but I'm sure you will have heard of his other alias."

Ted winced. He had worked out what was coming.

RIP Chapter 33

"My dad's look-alike pseudonym amongst my mates was Barack Obama."

Joe, Shane and Ryan guffawed with laughter.

Rob continued:

"If I could take a picture and send it to my mates pretending that we have met the real Obama and his bodyguards out here, it would be a real laugh."

Joe was happy to oblige and even decided to take a selfie with Ted to send to his buddies back in the U.S., tricking them that they had bumped into the ex-President on safari, chilling, now that he knew that his country was in such safe hands...Shane and Ryan did the same.

They had arrived at the mine dumps to do their morning check on the general whereabouts of the rhinos, so all disembarked. Neil and Ellie headed up the scree with the telemetry kit, while Rob, Tom and Harry scrambled up the path, as competitive as ever, betting on who would get to the summit first, while Ted struggled up the scree, feeling his age for once.

"Climb on board, old timer," he heard and before he knew it, Joe had grabbed hold of him, pulled him on to his back and was sprinting up the hill with jockey Ted perched on his back.

Joe and Ted were first to the top and instead of collapsing, Joe was doing fifty press-ups to prove how unaffected he had been.

"Nobody likes a show off," Shane laughed, and again before Ted knew what was happening and much to his sons' disbelief and amusement, he picked Ted off the ground and bench pressed him five times above his head.

The rest of the morning drive was equally surreal. They had to make an emergency stop to let some soldier ants cross the track in front of them. Three of them lost their caps on a particularly vicious overhanging thorn bush, which they had failed to spot, in their quest to find the rhinos. It was hilarious to look back and see three baseball caps hanging from the tree, almost like they were the fruit of the tree.

Rob had received replies to his text from his friends back home and the number of "likes" was stacking up, but more remarkably, Joe, Shane and Ryan had seemingly convinced and fooled their contacts, who had forwarded it, meaning that it had gone viral. A friend of a friend had even sent the picture to Fox News and CNN, but they had refused to run it as they had just interviewed Obama at the Lincoln Memorial.

It made them all realise how "fake news" and post-truth were so easy to instigate. It made them even more aware that you had to be wary of becoming too trusting or over-gullible.

The two groups of rhinos had moved a long distance since the day before, probably in search of water, as it had been incredibly hot. Neil was concerned that they were grazing and resting close to the boundary fence and not far from the nearest Venda village.

"If they are still here this afternoon, we may have to intervene," he had commented but they did not understand the significance until later on.

RIP Chapter 34

Siesta was first choice for all of them, as the effects of early mornings and late beery nights were beginning to show. They were also desperate not to miss out on any opportunity to go on a game drive.

When they finally surfaced, they found Christo, Neil and Jason deep in conversation on the sundeck. They had received a heads-up from Howard and from the Vetpaw team that the rhinos had been spotted even closer to the boundary fence. All were concerned for their safety.

Tom was surprised.

"Surely now they have been de-horned they are safe?" he asked.

"You would think so," replied Christo, "but you've got to remember that the Venda villagers are poor and starving and there's an awful lot of meat on a rhinoceros."

Ted and family were shocked and stunned. It seemed that the poor, defenceless rhinos were under threat from all sides. Even being de-horned and with a military bodyguard, they were still a target. Neil surprised them with his next comment.

"You can't really blame the villagers. If your family were starving, Ted, I bet you would do anything to feed them, even if it meant becoming an informant for poachers or being involved in killing an animal for meat. The rhinos are just a meal ticket for them and if it's a straight choice between a dead rhino and a dead child..."

He left the thought hanging for effect.

"So grab something to eat and we'll head off on a rescue mission for our afternoon drive. Oh, and we have a special treat for you all!"

As soon as they were fed and watered, Christo and

Jason boarded the cab of the bakkie. Neil and Ellie jumped on the back along with Ted and the boys. It was another stunning day with glorious bone-warming sunshine. Christo pointed out some threatening clouds in the distance, which reminded them of home.

There was no need for the telemetry this time as they knew their rough location. As they drove through the Reserve it was difficult to believe that these were killing fields and a war zone. It was so idyllic and unspoiled and amazing scenes awaited them round every corner.

Giraffes "hid" behind trees and stared them out. Prehistoric-looking wildebeest and warthogs were seen jogging through the undergrowth. Nyalas charged one another at the sound of the engine. Impalas bounced higher and higher to impress their audience. A huge eland stood imposingly, checking on their progress.

They got a particularly close view of a group of

zebras. A "zeal" or "dazzle" as Neil informed them. They were surprisingly large at close quarters, almost five feet tall and the stripes were distinctive and noticeably had different patterns.

"Nobody is sure why they have their stripes," Neil told them, "though most scientists think it's to confuse potential predators, as when they run it's impossible for them to identify a single animal to attack and they all become a blur."

It was true. When they finally finished grazing and ran off, it was an impressive sight, but your eyes took time to adjust and they had disappeared from sight by the time your eyes focused properly. The bakkie drove on and they finally pulled in at the end of the track, where the boundary fence started.

"OK, folks, stay with the vehicle, please, and no noise. We don't want to alert any potential voyeurs. We won't be long."

With that, Christo, Neil and Jason set off into the

Bush.

RIP Chapter 35

The next fifteen minutes were scary for Ted, Ellie, Harry, Rob and Tom. They sat in silence on the back of the bakkie listening to the sounds of the jungle. There were an added cacophony of inexplicable bashes and crashes. They exchanged glances, fearing the worst. All were relieved when Christo, Neil and Jason emerged from the entangled undergrowth, further down the trail, and ambled nonchalantly towards them, allaying their concerns.

Christo and Jason got back into the cabin. Neil explained what had happened as the vehicle headed back towards Venda 1.

"That was really odd," he commented. "We're so used to finding, calling and feeding the rhinos, that it seemed really wrong to be scaring them off and driving them away."

Neil described how they had thrown branches behind

the rhinos to scare them away from the fence and back into the comparative safety of the veld. It was vital that they did not realise it was them as this would have potentially damaged the trust and bond they had been building for the last few months, so they stayed down wind and at a comfortable distance.

The bashes and crashes they had heard were the branches landing and the rhinos stampeding away, living up to their collective noun of a crash of rhinos.

"We hated doing it, just as we were all emotional wrecks on de-horning day, but as Mutogomeli, guardians, we have to sometimes be cruel to be kind and put tough love into action. They should be safe now and I guess when we track them tomorrow, they will be miles away, probably up towards the mine dumps again. Job done and now it's time for your treat."

The bakkie drove on through the Reserve with the sun beginning to set and, in the distance, black clouds gathering and moving ever nearer.

Just to the left of Venda 1, the vehicle stopped and Christo instructed them to follow him up the hill, making sure they kept to a single file in case of snakes, which were commonly seen in this area. When they reached the top of the hill, he pointed out the caves in the rock ahead of them and motioned for them to follow.

Ahead of them in the white rock they could vaguely make out shapes, but it wasn't until Jason shone his torch directly on them that they came to life and they realised what they were.

It was Jason's turn to be their tour guide.

"These are paintings not engravings so they have been identified as Northern Sotho Art, probably about 1000 years old, possibly older. They used dirt or charcoal mixed with spit or animal fat, white clay and iron oxide for the red colour. If you look carefully here, you can make out the shape of a rhino."

They took it in turn to get a close-up view and were amazed by the detail and artistic skill.

"Some of the San Bushmen paintings date back a lot further. Artists are revered by the Venda tribe who believe they are called by the spirit world through visions and dreams to use their talent and fulfil their destinies."

Ted, as an Art teacher was particularly impressed. He was also disappointed that artists were not as highly thought of in the celebrity world of the modern day.

They headed out of the cave and climbed Venda 1 to toast the sunset, but Christo cut the proceedings short by announcing:

"Time to go folks. You are about to experience your first African thunderstorm to finish a dramatic, memorable day with a bang."

RIP Chapter 36

It was a race against time. This race was one they were definitely going to lose. There was no place to hide and nowhere to shelter, so they would have to head on through the storm, homewards as quickly as the rutted, potholed road would allow.

Rosie, their mum, had been terrified by even the most distant thunderstorm, but none of them had inherited her astraphobia, but this was something new. As the rumbles and cracks got louder, they could feel the tension rise and they gripped the rail tighter.

As the darkness increased the rumble became an explosion and they could actually make out the forks of lightning against the dramatic backdrop of the angry sky. They felt the first raindrops lash down and they were huge compared to the dribbles at home. Within seconds the rain was hammering against the vehicle and their skin and their so-called "waterproofs" were proving to be a futile covering against the elements.

They huddled together, laughing almost hysterically, and Rob burst into song, soon joined by the others.

"When you drive through a storm,
Hold your head up high
And don't be afraid of the dark.
At the end of the storm is a golden sky
And the sweet silver song of the lark."

They had all sung the song hundreds of times, but never in these conditions and certainly not in an open vehicle in the wilds of Africa. They had never felt more alive and yet closer to danger.

Just as quickly as the storm had gathered, it passed and by the time they reached camp it had completely stopped raining and the wind had died down. The sky had lightened, stars were visible and it was almost as if there had never been a storm, except those who had been on the back of the bakkie were soaked to the skin and were now literally steaming.

A change of clothes was called for and in the absence of a hot shower, a towel down and dry off. Ted was disappointed at the thought that there would be no braai that evening but was pleasantly surprised when he emerged dry and warm, to find the fire re-lit and the furniture already drying off in the tropical temperatures.

He was also delighted to discover that the Vetpaw soldiers had joined them and was looking forward to chatting to them and finding out more about their incredible experiences. Christo was briefing them as he strolled up to them and was clearly fuming; angry in a way they had never seen him before.

"There are three dead rhinos every day! How is that 'encouraging'? OK, it's down on last year, but still a national scandal."

Joe explained to Ted that the figures for rhino poaching in South Africa had been published in the newspapers and the headline enthused over a 10 %

fall in 2016, from 1215 to 1054.

Christo was still ranting:

"662 rhino carcasses in Kruger alone and a massive 2883 incidents of poaching. Thank goodness you guys are here. The war is escalating and the world needs to know. Hopefully your high profile will make news and people will start to sit up and take notice before it's too late and all the rhinos are gone."

With that he shrugged his shoulders and marched off to cook the braai.

RIP Chapter 37

Joe, Shane and Ryan were as positive as ever.

"It's really wonderful to have a new mission and such a positive one. Things need to change and hopefully once the word gets around that we are on patrol, it will act as a real deterrent so the Kruger malaise doesn't spread."

Harry, Rob and Tom joined them, looking much drier and less tousled than when they had returned from their stormy sundowners'.

Ted added:

"There's no doubt you guys will make a real difference here in Limpopo, but unless we do something about stemming the demand by educating the Vietnamese and Chinese, then the poachers will just go elsewhere. It's become big business. Only today I read about an auctioneer in Beverly Hills being arrested and indicted for smuggling rhino horn worth $2 million dollars. OK, it's against the law, but when you are talking about that kind of money, they clearly think it's worth the risk."

Ryan, the solutions man, was as matter of fact as ever.

"So we have a mission here. Other Vetpaw retirees can do the same in other parts of the world. Christo, Neil, Jason and co can do their conservation bit and that leaves educators like you to do their bit by informing would-be buyers and getting them to question the morality of murdering innocent animals for dubious medical reasons."

Christo had rejoined them and added cryptically:

"School starts tomorrow. There are a group of Vietnamese teachers in South Africa on holiday and I've contacted them and invited them to join us on the afternoon game drive and for tomorrow evening's braai."

Ted shook his head in disbelief. This was only day four of their African adventure and yet they had already had enough excitement and stimulation to last a lifetime. He had been hoping that he and his family would see some exciting sights and the wildlife and scenery had certainly delivered, but he had also wanted to meet some interesting people and try to gain some insight on the rhino and elephant poaching tragedy, but again it had already far exceeded his expectations.

Christo, Neil and Jason; Ryan, Shane, Joe and the Vetpaw guys; Howard and Gavin; Vietnamese teachers, there was so much to consider and discuss.

Rob had obviously been thinking about their last encounter with the Americans and was keen to find out more about them, and in particular the impressive array of tattoos they had adorning their arms.

Ted felt compelled to apologise and excuse his son's impertinence and rudeness.

"No problem," Shane answered. "The two most common questions we are asked are about our tattoos and what it's like to kill or see your comrades killed. Rob's question is better for a social occasion like this."

Tom was desperate to know the answer to the second question now, but would have to wait. Shane removed his T-shirt and took them on a guided tour of his tattoos.

"On my right arm is the Stars and Stripes of course and a Latin inscription saying 'De oppresso liber', the motto of the Special Forces we discussed the other night. On my left arm are a number of body tags with initials representing friends who have fallen and a representation of Odin in his warrior helmet with one of his ravens. Across my back is a bald eagle wearing a green beret and a poem which means a lot to me."

Ted and family read the words:

"People sleep peaceably in their beds at night only because rough men stand ready to do violence on their behalf."

"This last one on my chest is most important of all. It says 'Death before Dishonor'."

Harry was about to point out the spelling mistake and then remembered it was American English. It was clearly deliberate unlike his Internet favourite: misspelled tattoos - such as 'NO REGERTS', 'TOO COOL FOR SCOOL' and 'STAY STRONG NO MATTER WHAT HAPENS'. These are all real tattoos. There was so much to debate from his choices, but they all wanted to move on to the literally killer question.

RIP Chapter 38

Tom asked the ultimate question in his own inimitable way.

"Is it like 'Mortal Kombat' or 'Blitzkrieg' only for real?"

Joe acted as spokesman.

"Most ex-soldiers don't like to talk about their experiences for obvious reasons. I guess everybody's version is different, depending on their views and character. For me, I felt like I was in a cocoon, almost with tunnel vision, just focusing on my mission and remembering my training. I put on an Odin warrior's mask and tried to stay as calm as possible, especially as everything seems to happen in slow motion."

Shane added:

"You've got to believe that you are doing a job and

fighting evil otherwise you'd never pull the trigger and you would be the one to get blown away."

There was an awkward silence which Harry ended by cleverly changing the subject.

"It must be really challenging to settle back into society when you return home. Thank goodness for projects like this."

Shane took the bait and continued:

"I agree. It's well documented that post-Vietnam, Iraq and Afghanistan, returning servicemen received little or no support. They really struggled and suffered horrific post traumatic stress disorder."

Ted cringed at the very mention of the term. He himself had been diagnosed with it and received counselling and medication to help him deal with it after the sudden and tragic death of his wife, so he'd had a taste of it and shivered at the memory. Finding projects to occupy his mind and drive him forward so he didn't have time to dwell on the trauma of the past had proved his only coping mechanism. It was so much healthier than alcohol and drugs, though they were short term solutions.

"The fact that we are using our intensive training and skill sets is vital. We all feel that we have a mission and a purpose again, rather than earning a meagre few dollars, working behind a bar in Boston or ticking off the days on a retirement calendar. And who knows? We might even save a species while we're at it."

"How long will you be out here?" Harry asked.

"It's all up in the air at the moment because it's such a new initiative and has met with a mixed response from the media. Currently you sign up for two years, so we'll be here until 2019, but I for one will be looking to extend it and stay or find a similar project. I've fallen in love with Africa and as much as I love my country, it's not the right place for me at the moment."

Joe and Ryan nodded in agreement.

Ryan commented:

"I was involved in starting the project in the first place. We are a charity so rely on donations, but the mission is threefold. Firstly, it puts veterans to work. I lost myself when I returned to conventional civilian life and my combat-related skills were no longer relevant. This project has changed all that. Secondly, we aim to work closely with Rangers and conservationists like Christo, Neil and Jason - training them to protect their precious animals. Thirdly, we aim to support local communities and educate them so as to change perceptions."

Ted could see two of the arguments, but wasn't sure about one.

"Surely your combat skills are a danger in such a peaceful, idyllic setting. Are you going to train Christo to be a killing machine and Neil to be an Irish Martial Arts expert?"

The question was more forceful than he had intended.

"Our idea is to do the opposite. We want to be a peace-keeping force, deterring any potential aggressors. Telemetry works but imagine if we could train Christo to use radio tracking, heat sensors and computer technology, so he knew exactly where his rhinos were every minute of every day, instead of searching for them like giant needles in a humongous haystack. If we could fit the rhinos with the latest technology to monitor their health..."

His words were striking and almost prophetic as the next day was to demonstrate.

RIP Chapter 39

It was already day five of their Safari Spectacular and Ted had expected the novelty to have worn off and that he would have to drag his sons kicking and screaming out of bed, but that could not have been further from the truth. They were certainly tired, but there was no way that they would miss a game drive.

The family had settled into the routine of very early mornings and reasonably late nights, with a compensatory rest during the heat of the day and so were up and raring to go. Day five started routinely enough with a drive out to Venda 1 and an early morning climb to get a rough idea of the location of the rhinos.

The first group of three were tracked and fed easily enough, with Tom doing the honours by leading them out of the Bush towards the vehicle and their meals on wheels. The others proved slightly more elusive, but were eventually traced to a clearing down by the mine dumps, but there was an unexpected twist when they discovered that only two emerged; a cow and her calf. Rhino Bull 2, as his code name termed him, or Sterk which was his nickname from the Afrikaans word for strong, was nowhere to be seen.

Neil and Jason, who were leading the drive, exchanged nervous glances and Neil explained:

"Sterk is three and we've noticed a change in behaviour recently. He is always last to appear and seems reluctant to follow us and it also seems like he is being pushed away by the others. Our guess is that he is trying to establish himself and may well have taken himself off on his own to establish his own territory."

Ted was reminded of the rebellious, teenage years of his three sons, though he knew how lucky he had been to have come through unscathed with only minor skirmishes with alcohol to deal with, sulky responses to disappointing exam results or curfews during term time.

Neil continued:

"It's not good news for us or for the rhino. Chances are he will be constantly on the move. That means it will be harder to track and feed him. Worse still is that he will be a real target for poachers, as he may wander into dangerous areas. All his bashing and crashing makes him more likely to be spotted."

There was genuine compassion and emotion in his voice - which made Ted and family realise that it was more than just a job. The six huge beasts had become like family and no one was potentially in danger.

"The telemetry won't be any use if he's in the depths of the Bush or moving around, so we'll have to drive around and try and spot some solitary tracks."

It all sounded very exciting, but at the same time, very worrying.

For the next hour they were treated to countless views

of amazing animal and bird sightings. They travelled as fast as they could on the bumpy, potholed trails.

Neil and Jason stopped every now and then to climb down from the cabin to check tracks, but they identified elephant, zebra, giraffe and even hyena, before they finally had success.

Neil climbed up to tell them the news, but his face was white and was etched with concern.

"We've found Sterk's tracks heading east to west, but..." He hesitated and gulped.

"There are human tracks too. Stay on the bakkie and keep your eyes open. Jason is going to alert the Vetpaw guys and stay with you, while I go on foot, on my own, so as not to scare Sterk..."

He shuddered and without finishing the sentence headed off into the dense undergrowth.

RIP Chapter 40

After what seemed like an eternity, but was probably more like twenty minutes, Neil re-emerged. His expression told them that his search had been unsuccessful.

"There are loads of tracks and the depth suggests that he was running."

Jason voiced the question that was on everybody's mind, but nobody else was brave enough to ask.

"What about the human tracks?"

"I couldn't see any in the Bush, but in a way that's not surprising. Rhinos can trample their way through the undergrowth, but we would stick to any paths whenever possible. So if a poacher was tracking Sterk it would be difficult to tell. The only tracks I can see are on the road. Let's hope and pray that Sterk got away. But there is one other thing that is worrying me..."

He paused, almost as if wondering if by vocalising his concerns he was making them more real.

"I found traces of blood on some of the thorn bush branches and fresh drops along one of the tracks."

It was like a hammer blow to all of them. Ted and family had only been in South Africa for five days, but had fallen in love with both the place and in particular the rhinos. They couldn't begin to imagine how Neil and Jason were feeling.

Jason and Neil consulted for a few minutes in stage whispers. Neil then said:

"Right folks. We are going straight back to camp to meet up with Howard, Christo and the Vetpaw soldiers to decide on the best strategy. Let's just hope that we're not too late."

It was a bumpy ride home as Jason floored the bakkie

as best he could and everybody gripped the handrail tightly with both hands and sat in complete silence.

Christo and Ellie were waiting for them on the terrace.

"Excuse us please. I suggest you get some rest if you can while we try and work out what's going on and what to do next."

Ted spoke:

"Is there anything we can do to help? If you need extra eyes and ears, we will do everything you ask."

"Thanks but it's far too dangerous. If there are poachers out there, we are going to need our American friends with their AK-47s and military rifles."

The reply shocked and stunned the whole family and the penny finally dropped. This was a life and death situation, and not just for the rhinos.

Ted motioned to Harry, Rob and Tom to follow him to the rondavel, so they would be out of the way. As they trooped across, they saw Howard's Land Cruiser in the distance. It was heading at full speed towards the camp.

Somehow the family managed to sleep, or rather doze. They all had vivid dreams about wounded rhinos, gun fights and dramatic chases.

It was two o'clock when they all finally surfaced, but the camp was deserted and eerily silent. They made lunch and waited on the terrace for the return of the Mutogomeli. They were desperate to find out what had happened, but worried in equal measure.

RIP Chapter 41

It was three o'clock when the tranquillity was finally broken. The sound of an engine in the distance grew gradually louder, until they could make out the shape of the bakkie. It was followed closely by Howard's Land Cruiser.

Ted felt compelled to put on both parent and teacher hats and told his sons:

"No questions, lads. Let them do the talking. We'll be able to tell if it's good or bad news within seconds."

Harry, Rob and Tom nodded their assent and gathered on the terrace to await the arrival of the rhino cavalry.

As soon as they could make out faces and expressions, they knew it was good news. Christo, Neil and Jason were laughing and joking in the front of the bakkie. Ellie and Howard were obviously chatting away in an animated fashion in his Land

Cruiser.

Tom disobeyed his dad.

"Well, what happened? Is Sterk safe? Are there any poachers on the Reserve? Are you all OK?"

Neil, as ever, acted as spokesman.

"Whoa! Calm down. In answer to your questions the answers are: Yes, yes and yes."

Before they had time to assimilate the information he continued:

"As we were heading back out to look for Sterk, we got a phone call from the Americans. They had apprehended an intruder down by the mine dumps and had taken him back to their base to interrogate him."

The boys exchanged glances, each with a gory picture in their minds of exactly what the word 'interrogate' meant."

"They had also got a glimpse of a solo rhino who they presumed to be Sterk, crashing through the undergrowth, so we set off in that direction to check if he was OK. We presumed he must be hungry and hoped to entice him out with some fresh hay, but things didn't exactly go to plan."

He paused and his audience waited with baited breath.

"There's a water hole down by the mine dumps and what with the soaring temperatures and all his charging around, our guess was that he would be having a drink and cooling off, so making sure we were downwind we headed stealthily for the water hole, not wanting to alarm him any further."

Jason took up the narrative:

"Sure enough we could make out a huge shape in the waterhole which could only be a rhino or a hippo and we don't have hippos around here. It was scarily still and we all feared the worst. Had it been shot and wandered into the water to die? Was it seriously injured and bathing its wounds? But it turned out to be neither. There were some wounds and scars and even shards of thorn bush sticking out of its armour plated hide, but as he became aware of our presence and heard our familiar call, he raised his head and slowly emerged from the water covered in caking mud. We have never been happier to see a healthy looking rhino in our lives. He even followed us back towards the vehicles and tucked into some tasty relish with even more gusto than normal."

The smiles of relief, high-fives and hugs spoke volumes about what being a conservationist really meant. Ted and family found themselves joining in and breathing huge sighs of relief.

Christo changed the mood.

"Sorry to break up the party, but just to remind you, we have guests arriving in about fifteen minutes and

we need to be on our best form if we are to get our message across and educate Vietnam and China..."
"The Vetpaw guys are coming to the braai later so we can hear their side of the story and find out more about our trespasser."

As he finished his sentence, his phone rang to announce the impending arrival of his Vietnamese guests.

RIP Chapter 42

Ted, as a teacher, had done his homework on Vietnam and the Vietnamese. It was in preparation for meeting the visitors. One of his ex-colleagues and best friends, Mat, had immigrated to Vietnam to teach. Mat had married a Vietnamese bride.

Ted knew that the Vietnamese were highly educated, with 94% Literacy levels. They had consistently high scores and a top ten place in the academic league tables. Ted was intrigued to meet them. He wanted to find out more about their stance on rhino horn and Ivory. He could not believe that they were at the root of the poaching problem - as main customers and consumers.

Both visiting teachers turned out to have the same surname, Nguyen, pronounced Win. He was told that over a third of the population shared that same family name. Fortunately, for identification purposes, their first names were different; Chi and Dung.

They bowed respectfully when introduced to the boys and Ted was relieved that Rob didn't go for a cheap laugh about Dung's name. They explained that their names meant "man with purpose" and "courageous" respectively. Ted hoped that these meanings would prove to be prophetic.

Ted explained his son's names.

"This is my eldest, Harry, short for Harold, meaning army ruler; this is Rob, or Robert in full, meaning bright fame and the youngest is Tom, short for Thomas, or the twin. We're not sure who Tom is twinned with, perhaps Tom Thumb or Tom, Tom the piper's son."

The joke was lost in translation, but Chi and Dung smiled politely and nodded.

"Tell them what your name means, dad," Tom interjected.

"I'm Ted, which is supposed to mean wealthy guardian, so I'm not sure what happened there."

It was time for a sightseeing tour.

Neil asked Harry if he would ride up front with him in the cabin and take his turn on telemetry duty. Ted, Rob and Tom would travel on the front raised seats while Christo, Dung and Chi were at the back. Christo would be acting as the tour guide.

Jason and Ellie had volunteered to stay behind, to start the fire for the braai and prepare the salad, pasta and side dishes. They would welcome any of the guests who arrived early.

It was a stunning evening showing off the Reserve at its finest and they lost count of the number of times Chi and Dung gasped out 'nhin' which they learnt meant 'look' and 'wow' which was self-explanatory with no need for Google Translate.

They enjoyed the impala and kudu; laughed at the

behaviour of the incredible giraffes; marvelled at the wildebeest and warthogs; were impressed by the elands and zebra and were full of questions about the countless species of birds, ranging from hornbills and hoopoes to eagles and harriers. They seemed most struck by the huge tortoises, which it turned out were lucky and sacred symbols in their culture. They were clearly animal lovers and Tom couldn't wait for the braai to quiz them as to why they ate cats and dogs, if they cared that much.

The rhinos were at their most charismatic and cute and Chi and Dung took dozens of photos and asked Christo lots of questions, which Ted and the boys couldn't hear, but could tell were thought-provoking.

As the sun began to set they headed for the mine dumps and climbed the scree to enjoy the panoramic view. It was another clear evening and both the colours of the sunset and the stars that emerged afterwards were as awesome as ever. The beer tasted sweet and Ted was reminded of a hymn that they had sung at Rosie's memorial service, 'How Great Thou

Art' and a shiver went down his spine. As he glanced towards his sons, they were all lost in their own thoughts, but instinctively and telepathically, he knew that they too were remembering mum and toasting her memory.

The drive back was truly beautiful. The light in the sky highlighted the Bush in a way which Ted knew he would never be able to capture on canvas. He took some shots on his camera as a reminder of the beauty.

They were all starving after the excitement of the day and looking forward to chatting to Chi and Dung, also seeing their American friends again. It was to be a memorable evening in more ways than two.

RIP Chapter 43

Christo was late for the evening braai which was unusual when food was involved, combined with the hospitable nature of Afrikaans when guests arrived.

Neil told Ted that he had two lots of bad news when he had returned from the sundowners' drive. He had mumbled something about more members of the family being gone, which sounded very worrying.

Ryan, Shane and Joe had arrived and were holding court about their memorable day. It turned out that they'd had a call from Howard who had spotted human tracks while on his morning round, so they had set off on their dirt bikes in hot pursuit.

The tracks started at the boundary fence and were plainly visible on the 'main road' heading northwards across the Reserve. As they followed them, they suddenly veered off into the Bush, obviously alerted by the sound of the bikes. The three Americans had dismounted and encircled their quarry, cornering him and capturing him, quivering and cowering at their feet.

Tom the journalist wanted to know more.

"So who was he? Was he carrying a weapon?"

"He was clearly a Venda tribesman and he was unarmed. He was really terrified and offered no resistance as we escorted him back to the hunting lodge. "

Ted wasn't surprised that he offered no resistance. He really liked Shane, Joe and Ryan but they were impressive specimens of manhood and he certainly wouldn't have liked to get on the wrong side of them or antagonise them. He knew their brute strength from the piggyback episodes at the mine dumps!

Joe finished their account.

"He didn't speak any English, but by the time we

reached base he was jabbering away non-stop repeating "jammer, jammer", which apparently means sorry. We got Samuel, who works at the lodge, to translate. The trespasser's story was that he was on the run from his tribe who thought he had stolen from them and was taking a short cut across the Reserve to head for Beitbridge."

"Do you believe him?"

"It was definitely plausible from the way he was dressed, the fact that he was on his own and his whole demeanour. I doubt very much if he is a poacher. Shame really."

Ted presumed that they thought it was a shame from the combat point of view rather than the rhinos...

"So we handcuffed him, beat him to a pulp and handed him over to the local police."

The looks of horror around him meant that he could not keep a straight face.

"Just the last one," he laughed.

Christo finally turned up and looked ashen.

"Sorry to hear your news," Ted empathised.

"I can't believe it, Vince and Nola both dying on the same day."

Neil and Jason looked white too. They both clearly knew Vince and Nola too. Tom was too inquisitive to remain in the dark.

"Were they close relatives? Family members we heard?"

Ted cringed with embarrassment, but Christo was unfazed.

"Nola was 41 and one of the last four Northern white rhinos on this planet. Now there are only the three at the Ol Pejeta Conservancy in India left. Vince was a rhino in a zoo outside Paris who was shot three times and dehorned by poachers this morning."

"It happened in a French zoo?" Ted could hardly believe his ears.

"I know, unbelievable isn't it? The war on rhinos is spreading and all the press garbage about the positive trends in numbers is just propaganda and lies. We need to spread the word and educate the customers to stem demand."

He turned to Dung and Chi pointedly.

"This is where you come in!"

RIP Chapter 44

Dung and Chi smiled and bowed in their customary charming manner. They had proved perfect guests, listening intently to Christo and Neil, giving them the guided tour of the amazing wildlife Reserve.

Everybody had warmed to them immediately. It was clear that they were highly intelligent and educated individuals. But somehow they were still the 'enemy' and were now to undergo an interrogation.

Christo became chief interrogator.

"You've seen the rhinos now. Can you explain to us why your countrymen and others in the Far East want to see them dead? Can you imagine one of those beautiful creatures howling in agony after its face has been half hacked off or staggering around after being shot by those butchers?"

It was a very blunt and graphic question, but Ted and

family knew it was from the heart.

Chi didn't flinch at all.

"I feel I need to apologise on behalf of my country. I do need to assure you first of all, that Dung and I do not share their beliefs or theories. That's the whole reason we are here and we wanted to see for ourselves."

Neil was as diplomatic as ever.

"It's nothing personal. You must understand that, but we are all so frustrated and struggling to get our heads around it. If we could stem the demand for rhino horn, and for Ivory for that matter, the problem would go away and both those sacred animals would be safe.

"Absolutely, we are both educators by profession, so that's what we'll be trying to do when we get home. Spread the word and change as many minds as possible. I genuinely believe that most people don't know rather than don't care."

Ted offered his support.

"Haven't they started that with a story book in primary school?"

"Yes. A few months ago, your Prince William visited Hanoi and made a keynote speech begging people not to buy rhino horn and Ivory and he launched a children's story called 'I'm a Little Rhino' about an African rhino being chased and targeted by poachers. Now we need to get that book into every primary school to educate the young people and spread the word."

"That's all well and good but it may well be too little too late. By the time those children grow up there may well be no rhinos left - especially now as they are even targeting zoos and safari parks."

"Why do adults believe that it's OK to butcher defenceless animals that would never harm anyone, just to improve their love lives or show off their wealth?"

"It's more complicated than that I'm afraid. Traditionally rhino horn was coveted as an aphrodisiac or designer drug or to flaunt their wealth by using it to make ornaments to adorn their mansions. Now it's wanted for its so-called medicinal value."

Christo was enraged.

"But we all know that's bullshit. Rhino horns are keratin, the same substance as your finger nails." He angrily mimed chewing his thumb nail.

"Wow! The cancer has gone. It's a miracle. What are they thinking?"

Chi maintained his calm demeanour.

"We agree. But imagine your newspapers printed a front page story stating categorically that a prominent MP had been cured of liver cancer by taking powdered rhino horn. We believe passionately in the values of traditional medicine and so overnight demand went through the roof. That's why it's worth silly money. People with relatives with cancer are desperate and will try anything."

Ted remembered countless visits to the health shop, 'Holland and Barrett', when Rosie, his wife, had been diagnosed with the rare and deadly condition of vasculitis. He suddenly empathised.

"There have been denials in the papers since, but demand has not abated. We hope and pray that people begin to listen. Dung and I will definitely be doing a lot of talking."

Ted was struck by the enormity and complicated nature of the crisis. He was determined to discuss how best they could be rhino missionaries, before they headed home at the end of the week.

RIP Chapter 45

The evening braai started off on the wrong foot, with the interrogation of Chi and Dung. Everyone was feeling a little awkward. The atmosphere soon mellowed, when everybody realised that they were all allies, joined in one cause.

The friendships and camaraderie quickly led to a party atmosphere.

Christo introduced the Vietnamese to the delights of boerewors and the yummiest steaks in the world, washed down by lashings of Amarula and Castle lager.

Dung and Chi initiated the others with 'ruou raw' or 'snake wine'. It had a curious, lizard-like texture and taste. That was followed by eggnog coffee with real, raw egg.

Rob taught them the Katie Melua song, 'There are 10

million motor bikes in Hanoi' which confused Ted as he was convinced that it was about bicycles in Beijing. Rob also wound them up about barbecued pig, as they both had pet-pigs. They also admitted to having eaten dogs and cats for dinner.

Ted was thinking about his cat, called 'Nelson'. He hoped that Nelson's antennae didn't stretch as far as Limpopo.

It was late by the time Chi and Dung headed back to their resort hotel in Tshipise, but Ted, Harry, Rob and Tom were determined to be up early - rising with the sweet silver song of the lark to enjoy their last morning drive.

"Last day's last day" was a motto Ted had heard 63 times during his teaching career. It had usually meant an opportunity to enjoy some liquid refreshment. This was clearly after the little treasures had said their fond farewells and headed for home.

It was time for the pupils to tease their parents for a

few weeks, rather than their teachers. It also signalled an excuse for Ted's friend Sean to borrow his colleagues' car keys and hide their cars. He would also fill their school bags with shot-put or random 'gifts'.

On safari, 'last day' meant the last glimpse of all the now familiar sights, sounds and smells of Africa. The family were all determined to savour every second and fill their memory banks. This would help them get through the wet and windy winter days, which they had left behind, but to which they were about to return.

Their senses had definitely been heightened as each day of their adventure had passed and now the sky had never seemed bluer, the sun hotter and more invigorating and the scenery more picturesque.

Neil led the drive and promised to grant each of them one wish for their last day. Tom chose to climb one of the iconic baobab trees, both right to the top and, more memorably, inside the vast, hollow trunk.

Rob wanted to re-visit the mine dumps and try and beat his 'personal-best' for running up the scree slope to the summit. Ted was reminded of his piggyback trip a few days earlier.

Harry wanted to put a portfolio of pictures together, so was keen to take as many photos of giraffes failing miserably to play 'hide-and-seek', where their comical heads appeared above the tree line.

Ted was spoilt for choice, but decided that he would love to be in sole charge of the telemetry kit, act as Sat Nav to find the rhinos and then lead them out of the Bush with Neil.

It all went swimmingly and lifted his heart in an almost spiritual way.

When they got back to camp with the adrenaline pumping and a near glow of satisfaction, Jason told them that they had been invited to lunch. Therefore rest would have to wait until they were on the plane the next day!

Chi and Dung had given the invitation. They expected the group to join them for lunch at the Resort.

RIP Chapter 46

The Resort was a member of the Forever chain and was set in landscaped gardens. The restaurant was air-conditioned which was a real bonus for about ten minutes, until they all started to shiver and complain of frostbite.

Chi and Dung welcomed them and they had a tasty lunch of pepper burgers and fries, which certainly hit the spot. It was only 11 o'clock which seemed ridiculously early for lunch, but they were all starving and when they realised that they had already been up for seven hours getting fresh air and exercise they realised why.

There were impressive stuffed heads of buffaloes, kudus, elands and impalas adorning the walls which they would previously have marvelled at, but now seemed out of place and inappropriate. Their Vietnamese friends challenged them to a game of crazy golf, which they found surreal with wild monkeys wandering across their line of sight, but all really enjoyed.

As the group headed back to camp for their last sundowners' drive and braai, Ted quizzed his sons.

"Air-conditioning; restaurant food; hot water and crazy golf, that's more like we are used to. Do you wish I had booked the Resort rather than a rondavel with snakes, scorpions and no air-conditioning or hot water? You could have played crazy golf every day and worked out in the gym."

They rejected the idea unanimously, with Harry as spokesman.

"You know the answer to that dad. The whole idea of our trip was for it to be an adventure, rather than just a holiday. It's been that, and yet, so much more. None of us would swap for any 5 star experience or holiday anywhere else in the world. The only downside is...where are we going to go next?"

Ted was pleased to hear vocalised what he already knew to be true.

The sundowners' ride was as spectacular as ever with countless wildlife and bird life sightings and an incredible light show, as the sun set and the moon rose to reveal a sky full of stars.

Christo had invited all their new friends to a last night party braai. Serious debate on the afterlife, the fate of the rhinos and apartheid in South Africa were suspended for the evening. Instead there was karaoke with versions of Toto's 'Africa' and Paul Simon's 'Diamonds on the Soles of Her Shoes', as well as their favourite 'British Army' songs, 'The wheels on the bus' and 'Six white rhinos'. Party games were popular, particularly mobile phone favourites like the face swap app, eyebrow challenge and random drinking games - which Ted knew they would all regret in the morning when they had to pack, tidy up and head for Johannesburg Airport.

As the party drew to a close, Ted removed himself

from the crowd and sat quietly on his own, taking in the scene. His three sons were in three separate groups, laughing and joking with a real cross-section of disparate individuals who had all been brought together by a common cause.

Ted looked across at the crowd. On the one side Howard, his wife, Shann and son, Gavin, who ran the Reserve and made such a strong case for ethical hunting. To Ted's right were Christo, Neil, Jason and Ellie, confirmed conservationists who had dedicated all their time and energy to saving a species and protecting all wildlife. To his left were the Vetpaw soldiers with their totally different life experiences and views on life and death who were to become so important in the future safety and welfare of the precious rhinos.

Ted thought about the Vietnamese teachers, who were even now on their way back to Vietnam to try and change perspectives and correct misconceptions.

There are so many different people with such

different views, but all pulling in the same direction and prepared to work together to save the rhinos.

Ted was still confused as to whose view he agreed with, but he was sure of one thing. These were all special people who had formed their very own Special Force and he had the utmost respect for all of them.

He rejoined the party to enjoy their company for the last few precious minutes.

RIP Chapter 47

As the family headed for the airport, in their hire car, there was an eerie silence, which should have been unnerving, but was actually uplifting.

The morning had all been a blur. They had packed their dusty, dirty clothing into their back packs and suitcases. They tidied and swept the rondavel, changed the sheets ready for the next lucky arrivals then said their emotional goodbyes to Christo, Neil and Jason, thanking them vehemently for their hospitality and kindness.

They were each given a certificate with "Mutogomeli" as its heading, which meant more to them than any holiday souvenir.

Ellie was returning with them, to resume her teaching job, and Ted could only guess how hard that must be after such an incredible experience as an intern on the Reserve. He was just eternally grateful that it was her invitation and infectious enthusiasm that had brought them to this amazing location in the first place.

Johannesburg Airport was as manic as when they had arrived. Their arrival seemed like months ago. The 'Out of Africa' shop proved a hit with all of them as they hunted for presents for their friends and cat sitters.

They chatted contentedly on the plane, reminiscing about just some of their life-changing adventures and opening up about their personal journeys.

Ted shared that he was now more ready to face retirement. He realised that he had so much more to give; particularly influenced by the voluntary aspect of the project they had visited.

Harry had realised that there was more to life than money. He was now determined to make a real difference in whatever role he undertook, inspired by Howard and family.

Rob had been really affected by the soldiers and had decided that the army life was not for him, but he would find a mission and be more proactive and serious about life.

Tom cited Gavin as a key influence on him. He had been shocked how the press handled Gavin's story. Tom was all the more determined to use his writing talent for the good and avoid gossip, bias and propaganda whenever he wrote.

All were positive that they would do all in their power to follow the Mutogomeli motto to observe, research, understand, plan and change.

They had undoubtedly observed amazing sights, so now it was time to do more research and try and make sense and understand all the varying points of view they had heard, in order to make plans to paint, lecture, write, explain to friends and anybody who would listen and raise money to support projects like Wild Conservation and Ol Pejeta Conservancy.

They were all certain that they would return 'Diamonds on the Soles of Her Shoes' to South Africa. Their hope was that there would still be rhinos to observe and at which to marvel.

THE END

But hopefully
not of the
rhino species!

RIP Acknowledgements

My heartfelt thanks to all the following special friends:

To Ellie, who started it all off with a passing comment at a school reunion meal and then encouraged and enthused me to go, organised the trip, waited patiently at Johannesburg Airport while I was being interrogated, looked after me and made my adventure so special. She was an inspiration and such fun to share South Africa with.

To Francois, Neil, Jason, Frederick and all the interns and volunteers at Wild Heart, thanks for the welcome and please carry on with your vital 'Mutogomeli' role.

To Howard, Shann and Gavin, thanks for your hospitality and friendship and for being so open with me. Best wishes to Gavin in his new school and as a future Test Match wicket keeper.

To Ryan and all the Vetpaw guys who blew my mind and were such good company on the game drives and at the braais. I hope your stay in South Africa will be long and beneficial to both you and the precious rhinos.

To Barry and Peter who organised flights and airport transfers. Moxley and Co. is definitely, not probably, the best and most "stunning" independent travel agency in the world.

To Andy for using his 'Techie' talent, turning my words into the finished product so efficiently and selflessly.

To Sarah, Ann, Becky and Ruth, for their proof-reeding scills, which are vital to this project.

To Liz and the Place 2 Print team in Llandudno who did an excellent job on the marketing and publicity. They come highly recommended.

To Ruth and David, Mike, Diane, Holly and Florence, Paul, Michelle, Luke, Bethan and Emily, Becky and Ella, Lesley, Mavis and Rod and Diane who have encouraged me with this project and put up with my rhino lectures and obsession.

To Nelson for being my constant compurrnion and in loving memory of Lydia whose voice I heard and face I saw so many times. I miss you. R.I.P...

Finally - to all of you for buying this book, reading it and hopefully donating valuable and hard-earned cash to save a species. Worth every penny!

This is the fifth in a series. HDQ, TOL, AKA and LCR are available on Amazon and I can be contacted for questions, reviews and feedback on my Twitter account which is: @TimMoxley.

I really hope you found the book interesting and entertaining, but more importantly are moved by what you learned.

You may consider becoming a Mutogomeli, or guardian, by further donating to one of the following projects:

Save the Rhino
Helping Rhinos
Wild Heart Conservation
Ol Pejeta Conservancy

Alternatively, consider volunteering or becoming a 'Rhino Evangelist' to spread the word.

21703899R00114

Printed in Great Britain
by Amazon